OVER
AND
OUT

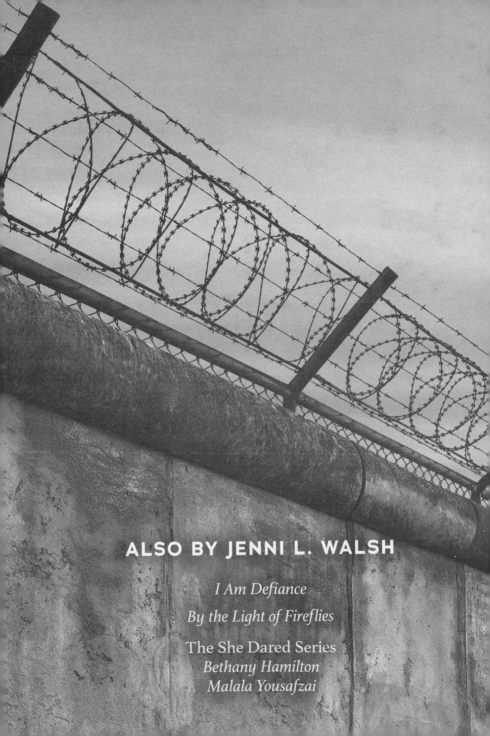

ALSO BY JENNI L. WALSH

I Am Defiance

By the Light of Fireflies

The She Dared Series
Bethany Hamilton
Malala Yousafzai

OVER
AND
OUT

JENNI L. WALSH

Scholastic Inc.

This book was originally published in hardcover by Scholastic Press in 2022.

The publisher does not have any control over and does not assume any responsibility for author or third-party websites or their content.

While inspired by real events and historical characters, this is a work of fiction and does not claim to be historically accurate or portray factual events or relationships. Please keep in mind that references to actual persons, living or dead, business establishments, events, or locales may not be factually accurate, but rather fictionalized by the author.

ISBN 978-1-338-77580-8

10 9 8 7 6 5 4 3 2 1   23 24 25 26 27

Printed in the U.S.A. 40
This edition first printing 2023

Book design by Maeve Norton

For those who came before us and
inspire who we'll become

Chapter 1

There are books hidden beneath my floorboards.

I was moving my bed because my only fountain pen rolled underneath while Katarina and I were doing our homework. At first, I tried to climb under after it, but my head was too big, no matter which way I turned it.

Not ones to pass up an opportunity to create something, my best friend and I decided to move my heavy bed—with our brain muscles. A much better choice for us than our actual muscles.

The sketching of a pulley system was quick. The putting together of it—taking rope and a wheel from my Inventor's Box and attaching it to the beam across my ceiling—took some trial and error. Actually going beneath our creation took some guts because neither of us was sure it'd hold.

We both remembered the go-cart we'd designed and built . . . that lost a wheel when we were halfway down the hill. And the slingshot that wouldn't quite sling at first.

This time it was "You go, Katy," followed by "No, you go, Sophie." Eventually, we did it together. And we were rewarded. As we retrieved my pen, the pulley held and my foot struck a floorboard. It made a hollow sound.

Katarina and I locked eyes.

Now we're side by side, on our knees beneath my tilted bed, the floorboard removed, and a secret cavity revealed.

Mama must've put the books there. Or someone who lived in our small two-bedroom apartment before us?

"Are they State-approved books?" my best friend asks.

My eyes train on a dark-colored cover. We're only allowed to read, watch, and listen to the books, newspapers, television shows, and radio programs that our East German government produces. "Hmm, I'm not sure if they're ours."

They *are* hidden.

"Well, grab one," Katarina prods. Her worried gaze shoots upward at the raised bed.

"Should I?" I look over my shoulder, expecting Mama to roll into the doorway, but she shouldn't be home for another hour. Monika is here, though. She keeps an eye on me after school. With so many working mothers, most kids go to an after-school program. But for as long as I can remember, Mama instead had Monika watch me. She's become more of a big sister than a babysitter. I'm twelve, after all.

I reach for the top book. It's about women aeronauts from history.

My mouth drops open. I'm already intrigued. Together, Katarina and I crawl backward from under my tilted bed, leaving it elevated, and lean back against my dresser. We begin turning pages, neither of us saying a word until she whispers, "Let's look for our names."

Sophie.

Katarina.

We find mine first, a woman named Sophie Blanchard. The first woman to pilot a balloon. She once ascended to a height of nearly four thousand meters. She crossed the Alps in her balloon. She performed for kings and all over Europe.

I'm more than intrigued now. I'm in awe. This other Sophie's life is more than mine will ever be.

I'm stuck living behind a massive wall. Actually, two walls. Two tall concrete walls separate the city of

Berlin into two sides: East Berlin and West Berlin. I'm on the east side—what feels to me like the wrong side.

The walls went up twelve years ago—to stop people from leaving our side, I've heard—and Mama says the walls will be standing for a long, long time. Some people can't handle being stuck here. They *need* to get out. They need freedom. I've heard stories of daring, unbelievable escapes . . .

Digging long tunnels *beneath* the walls.

Derailing a train to go *through* the walls.

Walking across a tightrope *over* the walls.

. . . but I usually only hear about the people who *don't* make it out—the ones who try to escape but are caught. Those are the people who end up as headlines in the government-controlled papers . . . to scare us not to try.

There was once this girl from school. Hanna and I were friendly, though not friends. Her brother tried to escape by hiding in the trunk of someone's car. It didn't work. Hanna's brother was never seen again. Her parents disappeared, too. Monika thinks Hanna's parents are in prison, even though they weren't the ones who tried to escape. And Hanna is different now. She still goes to our school, but she doesn't talk to a soul. She doesn't respond to smiles. She only wants to be left alone.

Mama says we should keep our heads down, too. She says it's not safe to draw any attention to ourselves. We should just try to live the best lives we can on our side.

Best lives.

I scoff at that.

My best life would be full of inventions and mathematics, just like Sophie Blanchard's—precisely the things the State isn't likely to let me do once my schooling is done, which is especially disappointing since my classwork focuses so much on science and math. Doesn't matter, though. Mama has a scholarly job she loves. She works in a lab. And because Mama has a job that's not in a place like a factory, I probably will have to work in one, despite how I have a mind for numbers. The math is simple for our family of two. One family member is middle class: Mama. One family member will be working class: me. It keeps a family balanced. If we're both in an academic field, then our family would be too middle class. Too . . . what did Monika call it . . . bourgeois.

She once explained my future to me in whispers.

You'll never be a scientist here, Sophie.
You'll be assigned a job in that factory.
If you grumble, the Stasi secret police will
find out.
They'll create a file on you.
You'll be spied on.
You could go to prison.
Everything you do will always, always be
watched.
You'll have no future. Not one you'd want
anyway.

Maybe Monika was just speculating, but she's one of the smartest people I've met. As I remember her words, all I know is that it sounded horrible then and it still sounds horrible now. I rub the goose bumps on my arms.

Across the room, my raised bed and pulley make a groaning noise. I eye it as Katarina flips through the book's pages. "I can't find my exact name. But look here," she says, "there's a Katharina Paulus, a performer, too—a parachute jumper. And look! She's also the inventor of the first collapsible parachute."

"I bet *she* would be able to invent a way over the Wall," I say, being sure to keep my voice low. We have neighbors, and our shared walls are paper thin.

Katarina asks, "What could we invent?"

"To get over the Wall?" I ask.

"Yes."

"But—"

"Just pretend with me," Katarina urges. "If we were the other Sophie and Katharina, what would we do to soar over the walls?"

I think on it. I rub my lips together. "Strap ourselves to a rocket and whoo—"

"A rocket?" I hear from the doorway.

I slap the book closed and yank it behind my back in a heartbeat.

Monika is standing a step into my room.

She laughs but then lowers her voice to match the tone Katarina and I have been using. "You don't have to hide that from me. You know that. But I will say that a rocket doesn't sound very safe."

Katarina smiles. "Neither does how that trapeze artist hung that wire and tightroped across."

"Or that," Monika agrees, taking a few perfectly

straight steps with her arms outstretched on either side. With exaggeration she falls to one side.

We all laugh, but my mind is elsewhere.

After the walls were built twelve years ago—oddly enough beginning on the exact day I was born, 13 August 1961—it's said that one of the very first people to flee was a guard who was supposed to be keeping people from escaping to the west side. That side is controlled by the United States, Great Britain, and France. That side believes in capitalism, where people can pick their own jobs, where there are choices of what food to buy and what clothing to wear, where the government doesn't own everything.

You want a car? Great! Go buy one.

That doesn't happen here. You want a car? Request one from the government. Maybe they'll let you have one someday. But fair warning: It could take ten years.

What does our guard fleeing our side tell you?

It tells me a lot.

Mama doesn't think I know as much as I do. I'm constantly watching and listening and adding more to the equation of why West Berlin > East Berlin.

I remember a few years ago when I first realized that the Wall separates us from the West but that it's the West that's actually surrounded by both walls. "Why?" I asked. "If the West is surrounded, why is it that we're the ones trapped?"

"Because the Westerners can come and go through checkpoints in the Wall to other parts of Germany," Mama said. "We cannot. We cannot enter their side. We cannot leave our side."

The Stasi police claim the Wall is to protect us. But I think Mama is right. I think the Wall is meant to keep us here. Not long ago, the State even started allowing people from the West into our side. If the Wall is for our protection, then why do their students come to our museums and theaters? Why do their people come to our restaurants? They just have to leave by the end of the day. Sometimes I watch them go with the worst kind of envy, wishing it were me who was going back to the West.

Mama says she's been there before. "A different lifetime," she let slip once.

I ask Monika now, "How would you do it? How would you get across?"

Monika was five or six when the Wall went up, but she says she remembers very little from before. "Only my grandparents," she once told me. "They are all I remember from before the Wall went up. I haven't seen them since. But I'll see them again."

Had she meant she'd try to escape someday? It seems impossible to actually do it. It's why we only ever daydream.

I wait for her to answer about how she would get across.

Monika smiles, but it looks like she's forcing her lips to go up rather than down. "Your mama will be home soon. Probably best to put all this away." She nods to the pulley system wrapped around my bed and to the book still behind my back. But then her brow wrinkles. "Do you think your mama hid those books there?"

I'm not sure.

Mama can be confusing. Or maybe the better word is *elusive*. I have always thought of her like a volcano. It's like her emotions and thoughts are kept below the surface. They're there, you just can't see them, unless Mama wants you to know what she's thinking or feeling.

"Well," Monika says, "whoever put the books there, it'll be our secret that you found them."

I nod, just as the rope gives and my bed crashes to the floor. The three of us jump.

"Looks like your newest invention could use some

tinkering with," Monika offers with a genuine smile. "We'll perfect it. Don't worry."

It feels good knowing Monika's on my side. And as she leaves my bedroom, she also whispers, "Going over by balloon sounds pretty dreamy to me, too."

CHAPTER 2

That night I dream of balloons. Big and round with yellow stripes. The balloon's basket looks more like a chariot. No less than eleven ropes connect the chariot to the balloon. I dream of being like Sophie Blanchard in one of these balloons. There's an illustration of her in the book. With almost everyone in the East wearing the same bland clothing, it's enchanting to see a person in this way. She wears feather plumes in her brown hair, which is pulled back at the nape of her neck, and a red cape draping behind her flowing blue dress. Her gray eyes sparkle. She's smiling.

I look similar, with my brown hair and gray eyes. I like that I physically resemble this other accomplished Sophie. I wish I could be bold, too. I wish I had Sophie's confidence to do more than dream, to push off and soar.

In the morning, Katarina and I meet at our shared street corner and begin our walk to school.

Our feet always slow when we're near the first wall. Sometimes we see people from the other side on their balconies. In spots, there are platforms where people from the West can see into the East.

The Wall itself is a funny thing.

We'll be walking down a road and then . . . there it is, a massive concrete barricade interrupting the street. The Wall zigzags. We have to detour before continuing on the same street. I think it's this way because the initial wall was built so quickly, in a single night. At first, it was wire fencing with barbed wire. Over time, the concrete was added. Then a second wall was built. In between, there's an area called the "death strip," consisting of watchtowers, trenches, snarling guard dogs, and trip wires.

That part of the Wall isn't funny. Not at all.

We stop walking. The first wall looms before us. As much as I want to be daring like the other Sophie, concocting a way over the Wall seems impossible. It's why we only suggest the most ridiculous ways, like strapping ourselves to a rocket. I say into Katarina's ear, "How else could we get over there?"

Katarina twists her lips. "Catapult?"

I twist my own lips and envision how it'd all work.

We're maybe ten meters from the first wall.

This wall is nearly four meters tall.

My guess is that the second concrete wall is a similar height. But between the two walls, there's that death strip.

I imagine myself in the bucket of the catapult.

The angle at which the throwing arm is pulled back would affect both how far I go and how high I go. I consider aloud, "I'm assuming our weights would make a difference."

"Yes," Katarina says, playing along. "Gravity would pull us down. A heavier weight would decrease the distance."

I nod. Gravity, tension, torsion. The three primary things to consider.

"We'd have to make ourselves as aerodynamic as possible," I say.

"Like an arrow."

We exchange a smile.

"Even your mama could do it," Katarina says.

Right. That's important. Crucial to an escape. I would never leave without Mama. She's all I have, besides Katarina and Monika. A catapult would be perfect for Mama. She could get from her wheelchair into the bucket. I say, "All she'd have to do is sit."

"Until the landing."

I cringe. "We didn't think about that part. But that assumes I even calculated correctly to get us far enough. I'd probably mess up the angle and we'd land right in a dog's mouth."

Katarina leans into my shoulder. I feel her head shaking. "Stop being so mean to my best friend."

I smile. Katarina is the best.

She adds, "We should go. They're watching us."

The border guards.

They don't like when people linger too long on our side of the Wall.

On the other side of the Wall, the West Berliners can stand on those platforms and gawk at us all day long, like we're in some fishbowl. But us East Berliners aren't allowed to do such things. We're the fish. And we'll never grow any bigger than our bowl allows.

Katarina and I take a step just as the guard clears his throat. I can't help looking back nervously over my shoulder. He wears a scowl on his face and a gun across his chest.

"We're going," Katarina whispers mockingly. "Keep your pants on."

"Your boring brown pants," I mutter.

She laughs silently, only her cheeks twitching.

But as we walk away from our daydreams and past one drab building after another, neither Katarina nor I feel like laughing anymore.

After school, I return home to find Monika already there. It took longer than usual to do the food shopping—and it usually takes ages to stand in line to enter the store, then to stand in line to get a number, then to stand in line to be called, then to place my food order, then to get a new number, then to be called to see if what I ordered is available, then to pay, then to take a third number to wait to pick up my purchases. I do this to help Mama so she doesn't have to do all that waiting in line. I do a lot to help Mama. Today, the time at the grocer only adds to my foul mood.

One look at Monika's face tells me one thing: She isn't in a good mood today either.

"What's wrong?" I ask her.

She only shakes her head.

Her demeanor is so different from her playfulness

and whispers yesterday. Earlier, I thought about asking her to help me fix the pulley and then explore what else is in that secret cavity. But she looks too serious for that. She's on the couch, one knee bobbing, her hands in her lap.

"Tell me," I say. Monika has always talked to me, saying more than she probably should. But before she says a thing, we always pinkie-swear.

She extends her pinkie now.

I take it.

We meet eyes.

Then still holding my pinkie with hers, Monika pulls me next to her on the couch. Only then does she release me, her head rolling back on the cushion.

"I think I've made a mistake. A big one."

"How?"

She releases a long exhale, while picking at the loose stitching of our couch. Her hand shakes. "You know this is my final year of school," she begins.

"Yeah?"

"I've been assigned a job for after I graduate."

I'm quiet a moment, afraid to ask. "To do what?"

"I'll be trained to work pharmacy."

No.

"I'm so sorry," I whisper.

Monika has always wanted to be a teacher. She's done everything right. She gets good marks on her classwork. She's been in all the Socialist youth organizations—the Thälmann Pioneers, then the Young Pioneers, and now a member of the Free German Youth—even though we linked pinkies the day she told me she never wanted to be in any of these groups. And Monika's family is large enough so that it's easy enough to spread out who's in which class. There's still room for Monika to have a job in either. But the powers that be decided: pharmacist.

Which is even more of a slap in the face to what Monika dreams for herself because pharmacist and teacher are *both* middle class. They could've selected teacher and kept her in that same class as she'll be in as a pharmacist, but no. They must need pharmacy workers more than teachers right now.

My heart breaks for her. Monika is eighteen. She's been given a job that'll affect the next *fifty* years of her life. She's had no say in it. None. How is that fair? How is that the world we live in?

I want to scream. For Monika. But also for myself.

The same thing will be done to me in a few years. What if they decide I can't be a scientist?

A new silence stretches between us.

"Let's get started on your homework," she finally says.

I don't think I need help today. "Okay."

I stand to fetch my schoolbag from where I dropped it by the door. But as I reach for it, I realize Monika never told me what big mistake she made.

Chapter 3

I wake to voices, angry and loud. I scramble out of bed, slipping on a wheel I'd forgotten to put back into my Inventor's Box.

I regain my balance and strain to listen.

My blinds are drawn. I'm not sure what time of day it is. It feels early. I still feel tired. Tired, but alarmed. What's going on?

There's a scream. It sounds like it came from Monika.

I race from my room and toward our apartment door. On my tiptoes, I look through the peephole. Men. They appear like ordinary men. Not uniformed guards.

One of the men peers directly at my door, and I hold my breath. He can't see me, I remind myself. But I can see him. His mustache looks oddly crooked, like it's been pasted on and not grown.

Who is he? Why is he here? And why did Monika scream?

Then I remember her words from yesterday: *I think I've made a mistake. A big one.*

I remember the whispered warnings she once told me: *You'll be assigned a job. If you grumble, the Stasi secret police will find out.*

Is that what's happened?

Is this mustached man an undercover member of the secret police? Is he Stasi?

The questions rumble through my head faster than the underground train that rumbles our apartment when it passes by. I press as far as I can into the door, my fingertips turning white, and try to turn at angles to see more through the peephole.

I can see nothing more. I can't see Monika. I run to the shared wall between our apartments and press my ear there. Behind me, I hear Mama's wheels coming down our hall. She says nothing.

But on the other side of the thin wall I hear "Fräulein Voigt, we have an arrest warrant." And "You're being detained for clarification of facts."

I don't hear words from Monika, but there are noises, as if they're holding her too tightly and she's struggling. Her mama and papa call out that she's done nothing wrong.

Then footsteps.

And her apartment door.

I run back to mine.

Mama shushes my hurried footsteps.

I look out the peephole but see nothing. They're already out of my small bubble. I go to the window then. The outside of the glass is dirtied from the air here, but it looks like the rising sun is shining directly on our street. I'm five stories high, but I know it's Monika I see being escorted from the building.

They bring her toward a windowless white van. It says *Bakery* on the side. No way that's true.

"Sophie," Mama says, "get away from that window."

I turn, my mouth hanging open. My hands are shaking. "They're taking her."

Monika must've complained about her job to somebody . . . and now they've taken her. Just like that. What will they do with her? Such a small thing to do. Such a big punishment.

Mama's shoulders rise, then fall. Her hands grip the arms of her wheelchair. "Come here."

I can't help one last look down at the street.

I'd heard of people being taken. But I'd never seen it myself. This isn't a girl from school's brother. This is *Monika*. And now Monika is gone, inside that fake bakery van.

A man is looking up at the building. He's looking directly at our window. I stumble back a few steps.

"What will happen to her?" I demand of Mama. "Please tell me."

"Keep your voice down," Mama begins. But then she says, "Monika is a smart girl. I think she'll be back."

"You *think*? When?"

"I don't know, my darling. I don't know. But we should keep our heads down, not draw any attention to ourselves, and—"

"Live the best lives we can," I mumble. It's more of a growl. "I know, Mama."

Mama has said it so many times over the years.

But what about Monika?

People disappear all the time. Some come back. Some don't. I wrap my arms around myself. Then Mama pulls me down to wrap her arms around me, too.

I don't want to be on my way to school right now, but here I am, on my way.

Katarina is beside me.

She keeps glancing at me. I'm unusually quiet. We both know it.

I'm thankful she's not asking me what's wrong. Sometimes I can be a volcano, just like my mama. Katarina knows I'll talk if I want to.

I do want to. A little; I'm worried about Monika, and maybe talking about it with my best friend could help. But I can't talk. Mama told me not to say a word about Monika being arrested this morning, even to Katarina.

"You never know who can overhear you," Mama says. "Trust me, I've lived through this before. I've lived in a time and place where there were eyes and ears everywhere."

Mama was referring to the Second World War. We live in East Berlin, but Mama grew up in München, during a time when a man named Adolf Hitler was in control of Germany. Back then, people would disappear, too, if they spoke out against this Adolf Hitler.

I keep my head down.

As we pass part of the Wall, Katarina whispers, "A cannon."

That gets a small smile from me.

I'd shoot Monika over the Wall first, after she comes home from wherever the Stasi took her. Then Mama.

Then Katarina. And her parents and brother. Finally, I'd soar across. A cannon is so powerful it'd be hard to mess up.

At school, I'm two steps into my classroom when my teacher calls for me. "Sophie," Frau Otte says, her voice low, "you're wanted in the principal's office."

"Me?" I ask.

My teacher has worry lines between her eyes. "I can't imagine why, Sophie, but you should go straightaway."

I stall.

"Go," she says. Frau Otte even nudges me.

My gaze meets Katarina's before I take a step. There's worry there, too. I've never been called to the principal's office before. And for the life of me, I can't think of anything I've done wrong.

I rub my lips together before knocking on the principal's door.

But Herr Anderson isn't the one who answers his door. A man in a nice suit pulls it open. I check the nameplate for the office. I have the right room.

"Come in, Fräulein Ziegel. You're right on time," he says.

The man smiles, broadly. He shows a lot of teeth. His mustache shifts. His fake mustache. I startle. He's changed from everyday clothing into a suit, but I realize it's the man I saw earlier during Monika's arrest, and I retreat a step.

I don't follow him, and he motions for me to enter the office. "Fräulein Ziegel, I have invited you in."

He has. Although it's less of an invitation and more of a demand, and I'm at a loss for what to do besides go inside Herr Anderson's office. My principal is not here. Nobody else is. Just white walls, a desk, and two visitor chairs. I look back toward the only way out, not liking being alone with this man, this Stasi member.

"Fräulein Ziegel." He gestures toward one of the visitor chairs. "Will you have a seat?" He takes the chair behind Herr Anderson's desk. He repositions a stapler and a cup of pens before he clasps his hands together on top of a folder. "I apologize if you were awoken early this morning."

My mouth falls open. He knows I know who he is. Or maybe he's trying to catch me off guard. In either case, he's won.

He smiles again, this time more tightly. "Were you and Monika close?"

I'm sitting in the middle of the room, but I suddenly feel as if I'm in a corner. The inside of my ear is itchy.

I don't move a muscle, save for a swallow I can't help taking.

"Monika?" I ask.

Even I know it's not a convincing response.

"Yes," the man says. "Your neighbor. The young woman who supervises you after school each day. You are familiar with her, are you not?"

"Oh yes," I say quickly. "I wasn't sure if you were talking about one of my classmates. There's another Monika here."

The man steeples his hands. "No, not that Monika. But now that we're on the same page, I'd love to have a chat. Just you and me. Why don't you refer to me as"— he waves his hand in a circular motion, as if conjuring his name from thin air—"Herr Becker."

I nod. I don't think he actually needs me to respond here. I can tell he has a mouthful he wants to say. He wears disguises. The only times I play dress-up is when I want to play games.

"I'm going to talk to you like an adult," he continues. "I think that's fair, don't you? Your records show you get good marks, you participate in class, you follow directions well." He smiles. "In my role, I am tasked with two main duties. The first is to stir out any conspiracies *before* they are even thought of." He taps his temple. "The second is to stop any injustices against our party *before* they happen. Ultimately, my job is to prevent people from harming our party and also themselves. Now, my guess is it doesn't come as a surprise to someone with your intelligence that Monika has been assigned a job that she's . . . disrespected. Has she shown any of this disrespect in front of you?"

"Disrespect?" I question.

"Bad-mouthing the job she's been given," he says simply. "Time and energy have gone into Monika's assignment. Her assignment is for the good of everybody. It's for the good of Monika. I wouldn't want her to be a harm to the party or to herself."

"She hasn't bad-mouthed," I say.

This is the truth, mostly.

He frowns, seeming disappointed with my response. "Well, I'll tell you, since I'm talking with you as an adult, that she *has* disrespected her assigned job. It's quite disheartening. In our society, there is no poverty; there are no homeless people. Everyone has a job. Everyone has a roof over their heads. Women with more than one child are given shorter work hours.

Women, in general, work the same jobs as men. Do you not feel all that is fair?"

"Yes, sir," I say. I won't deny there are many people who are happy with our way of life in the East. I simply am not one of them, not if I can't be who I want to be. Not if I'll be arrested if I ever speak out like Monika has.

"Let me ask you this," Herr Becker says. "Do you and Monika ever watch the television together?"

"Sometimes."

"Ever the news?"

"Sometimes." I've decided short, quick answers are the only way to keep my nerves from bubbling out of my mouth.

"Wonderful. Now, when you and Monika watch the news together, can you tell me the shape of the clock often showed while they are reporting outside?"

The clock? I wonder. Why should that matter?

He presses, "Is the clock round, or is it square?"

"Round."

"Ding, ding, ding," he says. I startle at the change in his tone. "You see, if you were to say square, then I'd know you were illegally watching the news from the West. Our clock, the main one in the city, is round. This tells

me you are faithful to our government. This tells me I can count on you, Fräulein Ziegel."

"Count on me for what?" I ask.

He taps his finger on the folder. He opens it. A photo of Monika is inside. So are other notes I can't read upside down. "Monika has recently come to our attention. As you saw this morning, we've picked her up for questioning."

He watches me. I pretend my face is made of stone. It's not easy. My eyes feel as if they could fill with tears at any moment. "Now . . . she'll be released within seventy-two hours," he goes on. "When she's home, we have no doubt she'll accept her new role and carry on with her life. I've done my job well, and I've addressed her behavior before any real injustices against our party have occurred. But as she does carry on with her new day-to-day, you'll be tasked with watching her." He pauses. I give him nothing. "What she says. Who she's friends with. If she does anything that makes it seem like she's further rejecting our way of life. You and I will meet regularly, and you'll report back anything of note."

Spy? On Monika?

No.

He asks me, "Will you aid the State in this manner? You'll be doing a service not only to us but to your dear friend Monika."

No, I repeat in my head.

When I don't respond, Herr Becker makes a *tsk-tsk* noise. He pushes aside the folder and reveals two more folders I didn't realize were underneath. He opens the second folder. I just about swallow my tongue when I see a photograph of myself. A recent one, from one of Katarina's and my walks to school. Fortunately, it's not a picture of us pausing at the Wall. There's also a piece of paper inside with a bunch of words. Before I can even try to read them, the third folder is opened.

A file on Mama.

There are various photographs of her. She's with a blond man in one of them, both of them laughing and smiling. I don't recognize him. My knees bump the desk as I inch closer.

"Your mother," he says, "has a comfortable job in a lab, is that not correct?"

I nod.

His fake mustache unsticks further, drooping.

"She's disabled. It says it here in her file. She had polio as a child and it returned in 1968, resulting in the need for a wheelchair. Your mother's current role allows her to sit while she works." Herr Becker rips off his mustache. He tosses it on the table. "However, it'd be a shame if your mother's job becomes too taxing or too tiring and she isn't able to keep up with the demands of her work. She'd be reassigned to another job. It could even be in an occupation that requires her to stand."

Mama can stand, just not for long. I have glimpses of memories when she could walk just fine. Now it's different. She'd never be able to do that type of job. Mama is older than my friends' mamas, too. She had me later than most.

Herr Becker says, "Disabled persons who are in need of help on a regular basis aren't suitable for the workforce. They stay with their families—although it says here, you have none." He taps her file. "Or they are placed in an institution, often in nursing homes for the elderly."

His warning hangs between us.

Mama isn't elderly.

Mama is perfectly capable of doing her job at the lab. Her brain is perfectly fine. It's only her left arm and leg that don't work the way mine do.

Herr Becker says no more. He motions for me to speak.

And I know what's happening. I want to spit on him, but all that'll do is get me taken away like Monika. Then what would happen to Mama?

"You'd like me to spy," I say. "But if I don't, my mama will be placed in an institution."

"Spy is such a harsh word. I prefer *inform*. You'll be joining an honorable group of informants."

He doesn't deny the part about Mama. Herr Becker shifts his focus to my file again.

There's a file on me.

This is all too much.

"I have a contract here," he says. "You are welcome to read it. But the main gist is that you can tell no one that you are working with us. No one. Not your mother. Not that friend of yours, Katarina. It goes without question that Monika cannot know."

Herr Becker outlines a few more points. We're to meet weekly. The location will be at his discretion. Our arrangement will terminate upon his discretion.

The only thing at my discretion is if I sign or not.

Signing means spying on someone who is like a sister to me.

But I know I have to. I can't put Mama at risk. This decision is actually *not* at my discretion.

"Here," Herr Becker says, "you can use my pen, Fräulein Ziegel."

I take his pen. And I sign.

CHAPTER 4

I return to my classroom, barely aware I'm walking, except for the echoing of my footfalls in the empty hallway. The doorknob to my classroom is cold to the touch. I shiver.

I try to quiet my first step into the room, but of course, everyone turns to look, including my teacher.

"Sophie?" she says.

I nod, as if saying *Yes, I'm back. It's Sophie. Sophie the informant. Sophie who is supposed to spy on Monika.*

Only, Frau Otte doesn't know any of this. It's as if she said my name because she wasn't sure what else to say upon my return. Now she adds, "We're on page twenty-seven. Please take your seat."

Frau Otte begins teaching again. Most of my classmates forget about me. Katarina doesn't. I feel her eyes on me.

I sit.

She's still looking.

That's big. Usually her eyes are on Anton. She's had a crush on him for years. Anton may be the one into archery, not Katarina, but it's Katy who's made *him* her target. Everyone knows it, except for maybe Anton.

I open to the correct page of my textbook, not daring to meet Katarina's gaze.

Still, she watches me. I begin tracing an old pencil mark in my desktop.

Katarina whispers, "Why'd he want to see you?"

She's asking about our principal, not Herr Becker. I turn my head toward my best friend, my finger still sliding through the pencil-inflicted groove on my desk. Katarina's brows are scrunched. She's not even pretending to listen to our teacher.

What on earth will I tell her?

It can't be the truth.

I can't risk Mama.

I stop tracing and say, "He got me confused with another Sophie."

"Wetzel?" Before I can answer: "Keller?"

Why are there so many Sophies here? I nod, which I know will lead to Katarina asking which one, so I follow it with a *shh*. I point toward our teacher at the front of the room. Katarina sighs but stops her interrogation. I hate that I've lied to her, the first time I ever have.

I stare at Frau Otte. She erases something on the blackboard. She writes something new. She flips a page in her textbook. Everyone else does, too. Including me. But I haven't heard a word she's said. My mind is on Monika.

If only she was given a teaching role like she wanted, then she wouldn't have spoken out. She wouldn't have been arrested. I wouldn't have signed my name to a document that puts everyone I love at risk. I wouldn't have a ticking time bomb hanging over my head. A week. That's all the time I have before this so-called Herr Becker will want to see me again. Will he show up at my school again? Will he tap my shoulder while I wait in the various lines for our meat and bread?

He'll demand I report all I've learned about Monika.

All I can hope is that I'll have nothing to report. Then I won't have to betray Monika after she returns.

I wake to sounds coming from Monika's apartment.

Has it been seventy-two hours exactly? To the minute? To the second?

I feel like I've been in a daze ever since Herr Becker made me sign away my soul. Katarina has stared at me and all but pleaded for me to tell her what's wrong. But I haven't. I can't.

I hear another noise.

It has to be Monika returning home. Who else could it be coming into her apartment so early in the day?

Mama's said nothing about Monika not being here after school. For once, I'm happy she's not the type of mama who constantly questions me.

In bed, I listen as Monika moves about her apartment. I doubt anyone else in her family is awake. Here, Mama is still sleeping. I should be, but I've barely slept since Monika's been taken.

I give up on trying to sleep. Instead, I tiptoe into the living room and to the shared wall. I press my ear to it. All is quiet now, eerily so.

I'm glad she's back. But now . . .

I press my lips together, thinking how it'll be better if I never see her again. Because *No Monika = No spying on Monika*. Except I'd hate if there was no Monika.

My gaze catches on our window. The blinds are open. Mama likes for the first sunlight of the day to hit her petunias. In the apartment building across from mine, there's a light on in one of the windows. In another window, the room is darkened, but there's an outline of a person.

I drop to all fours.

Out of sight.

A train rumbles underground, and I feel it in my palms and knees.

Had that person been watching me? Watching Monika? Or is that person merely standing by the window? It's a normal thing to do.

Mama sometimes stands in front of ours, laying a hand over her skin wherever the sunlight touches her. Mama's face is always slack, as if her brain isn't in our apartment but somewhere else far, far away.

"What are you doing, Mama?" I asked her once.

Her answer was simple: "Remembering."

I dared to also ask, "Remembering what?"

Mama didn't break her concentration from where she was staring. Her focus didn't seem to be anywhere specific—just the old building across from ours. In places, chunks of the brick were either darkened or missing from the bombs that were dropped on Berlin during the Second World War.

I waited so long for Mama to answer that I almost

gave up. But finally she said, "Not *what* I'm remembering. *Who.*"

My father? Could she have been remembering him? I've never met him. Mama has never even told me his name. For me, he's a giant missing part of an equation.

Angelika Ziegel + blank = Sophie Ziegel.

I have Mama's brown hair. My gray eyes, though, Mama doesn't have those. And I read that eye color is directly linked to genes. The charts never include gray eyes, however—just brown, blue, and green. With these limitations, I see my eyes as a very pale blue. And if the charts are correct, it's likely that my father also had blue eyes. What makes it tricky is that blue eyes are recessive. Even though Mama's irises are brown, her parents—my grandparents—could've had blue eyes.

Not that Mama ever talks about them either.

Mama wheels into the room now.

I'm still on my hands and knees.

"Sophie? What are you doing down there?"

She wheels closer. Her hair is sticking up in odd directions. I hypothesize that she's been tossing and turning just like me.

I answer her question with a question. "Sleep okay?"

She answers my question with her own. It's what we do. "How about eggs for breakfast?"

I follow her into the kitchen. I want to say how Monika is back, but if Mama was awake, she most likely heard everything I heard. And for some reason, she's dancing around the topic. I'm dancing around it, too, but because saying Monika's name out loud feels weird. In fact, it feels wrong—now that I'm supposed to be spying on her and I'm not supposed to tell anyone, not even Mama. Maybe especially Mama.

I don't even taste my eggs. I barely remember dressing and leaving for school. I startle at Katarina's voice. "I don't like that it's so cold today. It's supposed to be getting warmer."

I shiver, as if my body is finally acknowledging the chill in the air. Springtime cannot come soon enough. "Me either," I say as we walk down the sidewalk.

"Look," Katarina says. There's about as much enthusiasm in her voice as there was when she noted today's weather. Instantly, I know why. West Berliners.

Ahead of us, one by one, they step off a red bus. We

know it's them because of the color of their identification card covers. Theirs are green. Ours are gray.

"Another school trip?" I muse. There's a theater on the corner, my best guess as to why these other kids are here.

"Must be nice," Katarina whispers.

I nod.

Recently, there's been a treaty that's allowed people from the West to come to the East more easily. We still can't leave, but they can come here. It requires applications, a visa, and paying a fee, but then they can come across for the day. After, they leave, going back to their fulfilling lives in the West. Most of the time, it's grown-ups we see. But occasionally we see kids our age.

I stare longingly at their red bus as we walk closer. The last student steps off. They stand in an unorganized grouping on the sidewalk. I have the urge to yank on Katarina's arm and pull her onto the bus. We could hide, and maybe—just maybe—at the end of the day the bus would unknowingly ferry us beyond the Wall to the other side.

But no, I could never leave Mama like that. Chances are we'd be found out anyway. It'd mean big trouble for us, and also for Mama and for Katarina's family. And even if we did make it, we don't know a soul on the other side to take us in. We'd be refugees.

I take Katarina's arm, not to stage an escape but to navigate through the small cluster of seemingly foreign students. They are a sea of colors. They even wear blue jeans.

Katarina and I nearly match every day. We don't have many options at the clothing store to choose from. Our shirts and blouses are generally a pale blue or a light green. I close my eyes, giving myself a moment to daydream that I'm one of them, part of the throng in blue jeans. I'll enjoy the show at the theater. I'll return to the West. I'll finish my schooling. I'll become a scientist. I'm not *exactly* sure what kind. But that's okay. In the West, there's options.

Katarina gasps.

My eyes shoot open.

"What is it?" I ask her.

Her mouth hangs open like a fish's. She turns her body toward some students we just passed. Katarina points. "That girl . . ."

"What girl?"

I follow Katarina's finger.

My eyes meet the other girl's. A crease forms between her unblinking gray eyes. She's staring right back at us.

Katarina repeats, "That girl . . ."

. . . *Looks just like me.*

CHAPTER 5

Two chaperones clap their hands, calling the attention of their students.

The look-alike girl and I still lock eyes.

A friend tugs on her arm.

The girl resists, but her friend is persistent.

Before I know it, Katarina and I stand on the empty sidewalk.

"You saw her, too. You saw her, Sophie, didn't you? I'm not losing my mind?"

"I saw her," I say, my voice shaky. But who was that? Who I am feels like a huge question mark. But I can't help thinking . . . that girl is part of my equation, too.

"She has your face," Katarina says. "Your same nose."

I touch it. Flat on the very tip.

"Freckles, gray eyes." Katarina waves her hand over my face. "The only difference is her hair is a lot lighter than yours."

My head slowly bobs, acknowledging everything Katarina says—*agreeing* with everything my best friend says.

"She's around our age, too. Sophie, who *was* that?"

I swallow. "I don't know."

Katarina is staring at me. An older man passes us on the sidewalk. We're alone again. Katarina bites her lip.

"Say it, Katy. Just say what you are thinking."

"I thought you said you didn't have any family besides your mama?"

"I said my mama has never once talked about any family."

"Oh," Katarina says.

"Yeah."

I touch my nose again. A chill makes its way down the back of my blouse. I look toward the Wall. I can't see it from here. There are tall buildings in the way. But I know it's there. Just like I now know there's a strong probability I have family on the other side that I can't see. That I've never known about. That means, if we ever did make it to the West, we would *not* be refugees. And that's one of the reasons Mama has told me about why she'd never escape: "We have no one over there to take us in, Sophie."

But was she being truthful?

Katarina speaks carefully and slowly. "You truly looked, like, so alike. Close enough to be"—she pauses—"sisters."

Sisters?

"No." I shake my head, the fierceness of the motion and the denial growing. "My mama would've told me if I had a sister. If she had another daughter. She couldn't keep that from me, right? It'd be so wrong."

"So wrong." Katarina touches my arm. "Not a sister, then. But maybe a cousin?"

I stop shaking my head and now press my fingers to my temples. I close my eyes. *A secret cousin.* It feels more possible than the idea of having a secret sister. It hurts less, too.

"What if," Katarina begins, "your mama doesn't even know about her? You were born here. What if that girl was born over there, after the Wall went up?"

That feels even more possible, a viable hypothesis. That gives me hope. It still angers me, though. It means Mama has a sister. I have an aunt. And wouldn't Mama have known if her sister was pregnant? Babies don't happen overnight.

I have so many questions I feel dizzy. The sidewalk begins to swirl around me.

Katarina tightens her grip on my arm. "We should go. We're going to be late to school."

School?

The word feels foreign, like my brain is too full to comprehend even such an ordinary and common word. I say, "I can't go to school right now."

But even as I say it, a thought chases my words: *If I don't go to school, will Herr Becker become suspicious of me and think I'm up to something?*

I don't want that.

I nod to Katarina. "Never mind. Let's go."

"Oral hygiene is of great importance," our health teacher says. We have this same lecture word for word every year. Even if this information *was* groundbreaking, after the morning I've had my attention is not on my teeth.

It's on that girl.

It's on Monika being back.

It's on Herr Becker.

It's on the fact he has files on me and everyone I love.

I wish I had been able to read what was written, but it was all upside down for me.

I flip my worksheet around. I focus on the words,

trying to read them wrong-side up. It feels like a good thing to practice. I'll be ready next time, not that I want there to be a next time.

Katarina clears her throat, trying to get my attention. No doubt she's wondering what I'm doing. I pretend I don't hear her. I raise my head, focusing on my teacher.

"Flossing, brushing, and rinsing with mouthwash is an ideal approach to ensure the best dental health possible and to prevent cavities."

Cavities.

Hearing that word awakens something in my brain. I tap against my desk until . . . it comes to me:

I never fully searched the secret cavity under my bed.

Katarina and I only explored the first book about women aeronauts before Monika told us to put everything away before Mama got home.

In the morning, Monika was arrested.

Then Herr Becker made me a spy.

My thoughts have been on all *that*. Until today, when I saw *her*. Whoever that girl is. No wonder my mouth feels dry and my head is fuzzy, as if I've run a race and still haven't gulped down any water.

There hasn't been an opportunity to explore the cavity under the floorboards again. But what if Mama has photos or other family secrets hidden in there? It's all I can think about until school lets out.

I'm breathless by the time I climb the five stories to my apartment door.

"Hello?" I call as I enter, shrugging off my schoolbag. It lands with a *thud*.

No answer. Thank goodness.

I remind myself *No Monika = No spying on Monika*.

Beside my bed, I drop to my knees. I wring my hands together, listening for any sounds. Mama's not here. I have no clue if Monika will be over to watch me or if her arrest has changed things.

We never perfected my pulley. No way I'm trying that again, especially by myself. I push my bed with every bit of strength I have. My socks slip against the floor. Taking them off helps. Slowly, my bed moves enough where I can reach an arm and shoulder beneath to pry open the floorboard and remove what's inside.

One book.

Two.

Three.

Four.

I slide myself and the books free from underneath

my bed. I run a hand over the cover of the women aeronauts book, remembering the stories of Sophie Blanchard inside, and then I set it aside.

Could I be like that Sophie? Daring and brave?

The remaining books are in a language I can't read. Still, I thumb through the first of the thick books. The flipping of pages abruptly stops, the momentum interrupted by a new force: a small cluster of folded papers.

I jump back and drop the book, the papers landing on the floor in front of me.

"Mama," I breathe to myself. "Did you put these here?"

I look over my shoulder at my empty doorway—and back at the clues awaiting me.

Or at least they feel like clues.

They could be about so much: Mama's past, the girl from this morning, a family kept hidden from me . . .

With shaking hands, I open the first to reveal a newsprint:

ANTI-HITLER STUDENTS REMEMBERED

There's a line of three photos within the rows of text. Two boys and a girl. My eyes catch on the girl. My eyes go big at her name. Sophie Scholl.

Sophie.

When I came across Sophie Blanchard's name in the aeronaut book, my stomach did a dance of excitement at the coincidence. This feels different.

Intentional.

This article was clipped, folded small enough to fit in a wallet, and kept for a reason. I notice a marking next to Sophie's name. Now I see it's in the shape of a heart, drawn in.

Slowly, I set it aside.

The next item appears to be the back of a small photograph folded in half, hiding the image. I wring my hands together, nervous to reveal *who* or *what* is inside.

It's a younger Mama and a man I don't recognize. Yet he does seem familiar, in a way.

Mama's in a veil and a simple dress. She's holding a bouquet of petunias. They are one of the only flowers I know the name of, one of the few flowers that Mama seems to keep around the apartment, along with blue cornflowers and bluestars.

The man beside her is in a black tuxedo.

They're both smiling.

His arm is around her.

Is this Mama's wedding photo? Could this man be my father?

I scrutinize him—his blond hair, his blue eyes, his smile—and I realize it's not the first time I've seen him. He was in the photograph I saw in Mama's file that Herr Becker keeps.

Why did Herr Becker have that photo?

And maybe a better question: Why was this photo hidden under my bedroom floorboards?

CHAPTER 6

There are other pieces of paper and scraps, too.

Along with the news clipping and the photograph, there is a grocer list, ticket stub, and a receipt. Those last three don't seem to go with the first two, but everything is folded in a similar way, as if all kept together in the same small space, like a coin purse or wallet.

I put the clues back into the book. Back into the cavity. I push my bed back into place until I'm breathless.

I was tempted to put the photograph under my pillow, but I didn't. Mama hid the photograph in a safe place for a reason—and I don't often question her. The times I do, she does one of two things: She'll either press her lips together and say nothing. Or she'll talk around things. She'll say something like "There's always something to question, isn't there, darling?"

But should I question her now about what I've found?

Is the man in the photograph my father, the other half of the equation that makes me *me*?

And who is Sophie Scholl?

I slump onto my bed and wipe dust from my knees. I release a long, controlled breath. Up until seventy-two hours ago, my life had felt routine, barely ever a surprise. And now . . . now everything has been turned upside down and shaken.

I stand to retrieve my schoolbag, my homework awaiting me inside. It's something normal to do. But as soon as I turn into the hallway, I run straight into Monika.

"Sophie, there you are. Sorry I'm late."

I shake my head, which goes against me saying, "It's okay. I didn't hear you come in."

"Oh? Well, here I am," she says flatly.

Here she is. Back from wherever the Stasi took her. On the outside, Monika looks tired but like her usual self. No marks, no bruises. But I wonder how her insides feel. Her eyes look like they could fill with tears at any moment.

I lick my lips and drop my gaze to my shoes.

She reaches her pinkie toward me.

Monika wants to tell me something.

I'm supposed to take it.

But I don't want to.

I don't want to know what she has to say. I *can't* know.

"Sophie," she presses, and hooks my pinkie with hers. If I yank myself free, it could hurt her feelings. She may want to know why I did it. I could say I'm scared. It's true. But I'm afraid I'll say the wrong thing or do the wrong thing. So I stand here and watch her chest rise and fall before she says softly, "They kept me in a cell. All by myself. It was pitch black. I didn't know how long I'd be there. They told me nothing." She lets out a sad-sounding noise. "Besides how I shouldn't tell anyone any of this."

I begin shaking my head again. My words come out barely more than a whisper. "Then don't."

When Monika doesn't respond, I raise my head to see her face. She's the one looking away now. Her bottom lip is between her teeth.

"You're right," she says, unlinking our pinkie promise. "I shouldn't. You're too young to hear this."

No, I think. I'm not too young. I'm too afraid. Herr Becker will ask me what she's said to me. I don't want there to be anything to tell him. Already, she told me something she wasn't supposed to. "I should do my homework," I say. "I don't need any help today with it."

"Wait." Monika grabs my arm. "I was late today because—"

"It's okay, Monika."

"They took me straight to the pharmacy after . . ." She trails off. The sadness in her eyes hardens. "They wanted me in training right away. I'm only telling you this because today will be my last afternoon with you. I'll be doing longer trainings beginning Monday."

It feels like I've been punched in the stomach. I'm glad she still grasps my arm because I need that support from her. She's been spending afternoons with me for as long as I can remember. I knew she'd stop babysitting me eventually. It's not as if I even *need* her here anymore, and Monika was always going to have a job soon. But after everything else I've learned over the past few days, this news is yet another kick in the teeth.

"I'll still see you, Sophie. I still live right next door. We'll still hang out. We'll still have our talks. I'll always be here for you."

I nod; my mouth is too dry to speak.

She adds, "I'm not going anywhere."

I cough. That may not be true, not if Herr Becker suspects her of stepping out of line again. "I think the pharmacy will be good for you," I say. I hate lying, but I power through. I need to encourage her to do what's expected of her, even though I don't blame her—not even a little. "I'm happy for you. I think you'll really like working as a pharmacist."

Monika narrows her eyes. "Why are you saying this?"

"Because it's what I think?" I say it as a very unconvincing question instead of a confident statement.

"You're acting strange, Soph."

I am. But I'm also confused and scared and have a zillion questions. Oh, and exhausted. I'm so tired, too.

I sleep until nearly noon. Fortunately, I have off from school today, I've already done my homework for the weekend, there isn't a Young Pioneer meeting today, and I have nothing else planned, beyond lying on the couch and watching television.

I bet there'll be reruns on of *Today at the Krügers*. It's an adult drama that Mama lets me watch sometimes. Though, do I really want to be watching that? The show is about a family, three generations worth of grandparents, parents, and kids. And I currently have a big question mark about my own family. Oh, and one of the kids' names is Monika.

I think I'll pass on watching after all. Not when Monika is already on my mind too much.

Five days.

There's only five days until Herr Becker wants to see me again.

I sink deeper into my covers.

I have no clue what I'll say to him.

"Sophie?" I hear Mama calling. "You up yet?"

"No." I swing my feet out of bed. The floor is cold under my bare feet. I find my slippers and a robe.

In the kitchen, Mama is standing at the stove. I smell sausage. The muscles in her legs are trembling. Hurrying, I get her wheelchair and put it behind her legs just as she turns to look for it.

She drops like a sack of potatoes. "Thank you, Sophie."

I repeat my name in my head.

Sophie.

Now that I found the newsprint, I'm curious about Sophie Scholl and why Mama kept the clipping. It was obviously important enough to hide it. It makes me wonder ... "Mama," I begin, slumping into a chair at the kitchen table, "where did my name come from? You've never told me."

Mama wheels toward the fridge. "It's pretty, isn't it?"

"Sure," I say, drawing out the word. Mama is dodging my questions like she usually does—and usually I'd let her. But I can't help thinking again that sharing a name with Sophie Scholl is more than a coincidence. "Was I named after anyone?"

The cool air of the freezer swirls around Mama. Her hand is clutched on the door. Slowly, she closes it and turns her chair to face me.

I hold my breath, expectation coursing through me. Is Mama going to answer me? I will her to go on.

She does. "A girl I once knew," Mama says in a soft voice. "She was my best friend when I wasn't too much older than you are now." She pauses, then says almost to herself, "In fact, you're the same age Brigitte was when . . ."

Brigitte? It's the first I've ever heard that name before, but I want Mama to finish what she was saying. "*When* what, Mama?"

Mama's lips are pressing again. She sighs. "When the Sophie I once knew died."

I stop myself from asking *Sophie Scholl?* because then

Mama will know I found her secret stuff. Instead, I say, "How?"

"It was during the war. Sophie was very brave and wasn't willing to accept what Adolf Hitler was doing. So, along with her older brother and some of their friends, they wrote leaflets that spoke out against Hitler and the Nazi Party. They called themselves the White Rose resistance. I helped," Mama said. "But it was mostly the Scholls."

The Scholls. She said it.

"They made a big difference. They gave people hope. They stood up for what they believed in." She takes a deep breath. "But then Sophie was caught and . . ."

"I'm sorry, Mama."

"Me too. War is ugly. Adolf Hitler was ugly."

"But Sophie was brave."

Mama smiles. "Yes. And yes, you are named after her. You're brave, too, darling."

Am I?

The past couple of days have made me think more than ever that I am not.

I swallow, wanting to be brave now. I want to ask Mama who Brigitte is. I want to tell her about the girl

I saw on the street. I want to confess I found a photograph of her and my maybe father. I want to know
more about him. I want to confide in her about Herr
Becker.

But just as I'm working up the courage to ask about
Brigitte, there's a knock at the door.

CHAPTER 7

Mama's eyes narrow. My heart bangs in my chest.

"Are you expecting anyone?" Mama asks.

I shake my head.

I certainly don't feel brave right now. How can I when Mama presses a finger to her lips?

But it's not as if we were talking about anything wrong. Or at least I didn't think we were.

Whoever is outside our door knocks again.

"Stay here," Mama says. She wheels from the kitchen to the living room.

I wait, holding my breath.

"Hello, is Sophie in?"

I exhale. It's Katarina.

"Sophie," Mama calls. I go to greet my friend. She asks if I want to go collecting. By that she means going out to look for bottles, scrap metal, paper bags, books, glasses, and so on. The government encourages it and pays kids for the stuff they turn in for recycling. Typically, we turn in some. But we also keep the coolest things for my Inventor's Box, like the pulley and an arrow head we once found.

Soon, I've changed from my pajamas and I'm heading outside. It's still cold enough to need a coat. Beside me, Katarina has her own buttoned to her chin. I can practically feel her vibrating with questions. "I wanted to ask my mama about the girl, but I didn't," I say, offering up something I can share. I take a bite of the sausage on thin white bread I took with me for our walk.

She twists her lips, not hiding her disappointment, as she pushes a trolley cart.

"But I found more," I say, swallowing my bite, "in that secret hiding spot. I looked in it again, and there was a newsprint about a girl named Sophie Scholl, who was a hero of the Second World War. I worked up the courage to ask my mama where my name came from, and I'm named after that Sophie." We're about to pass a man and woman and I lower my voice. "There was also this photo of my mama with a man, who may or may not be my father? You knocked before I could ask her anything else."

"Sorry," she offers. Her face glows in response to all the

new information. "I was dying to know about that girl."

I sigh. "Sorry."

Without realizing it, we've passed the theater where we first saw *her*, and the Wall looms before us.

"A hot-air balloon," Katarina says, picking up our game of how we'd get across, "just like your Sophie Blanchard."

I finish the last of my sandwich. "Or we'd get really, really high on an apartment building and parachute over like your Katharina."

We both smile at the possibilities, as absurd as they are, and I allow myself to picture Sophie Blanchard's balloon, big and round with yellow stripes—and also filled with hot air. I learned in class hot air rises because it's lighter than the cooler air around it. Getting our hands on a torch to heat the inside of a balloon doesn't seem likely.

Katarina asks, "Do you think that girl is over there, talking and thinking about us—about *you*—just like we are about her?"

At this portion of the Wall, there's a viewing platform on the West's side. People often stand there looking into our side, even all these years after the walls have been between us. Today, there's an older woman. Her expression is too far away to see, but it looks as if she holds her fist over her heart. Is she waiting for someone? Will they use sign language or pantomime to each other? Or is it enough to simply see each other?

It doesn't feel like enough to have only seen that girl, that possible cousin of mine, a single time.

"Katy," I begin.

She stops mid-bend from collecting a discarded newspaper. "Never before has someone said my name so seriously. What is it?"

There's a guard up ahead, so I turn us around, still following the Wall but now going in a different direction. This isn't a conversation to have near him. I imagine my words having a smell attached to them. A conspiratorial scent, where he'll catch a whiff and know we're talking about taboo things: like how I sincerely want to get us over the Wall.

"The rocket, catapult, cannon, balloon, parachute," I say. "Part of the reason why we've come up with all those silly ways is because there's never been anyone on the other side to take us in once we get there, right?"

"Right," she says, "along with how it'd be nearly impossible to actually escape."

That reminder from Katarina almost squashes what

I want to say next, but then I remember Sophie and Sophie and how they never would've achieved great things if they gave up. "Us escaping has never been a real possibility. But what if it is, Katy? What if that girl really is my family? What if there's more of them? My mama mentioned someone named Brigitte today. I don't know who she is either. Only that she was around our age during the war. Plenty old enough to be that girl's mother. What we really need is more information on all of them."

Our next steps are taken in silence. We walk until the Wall blocks our right and the canal is ahead of us and to the left. There's nowhere else to go. Wordlessly, we turn around. Katarina catches my eye then, and she doesn't have to say it for me to understand what she's thinking. *It's time to go home. It's time for me to harness my inner Sophie Scholl and Sophie Blanchard and have a real conversation with my mama.*

My dread of that inquisition grows as I shake off the cold in the lobby of my apartment building.

I eye the paternoster. I generally choose the stairs instead. To be honest, the elevator lift intimidates me, despite that I'm endlessly interested in how it works.

I once observed it for an hour. The lift is always in motion. It never comes to a stop. Passengers step into and out of either the "up" or "down" side. There is no door on either compartment. There isn't a button to select a floor. It moves slowly. I counted and measured that it travels a third of a meter every second. The lift rises and lowers on a chain that loops around and around a gear at the top and at the bottom. And it doesn't fit more than one person at a time. Though I've ridden on Mama's lap before, my eyes squeezed closed as we rolled on.

It's not recommended for people in wheelchairs, or the elderly or children, but Mama has getting onto the paternoster down to a science.

I decide to practice being brave today and time my approach, watching the compartment lift, lift, lift until the floor of the compartment is nearly level with the floor of our lobby. Then I dash forward, watching my steps so I don't trip.

I'm on.

And on my way up.

I count to forty.

Then I watch as the fifth floor slowly appears as the compartment rises. Again, when the floors are even, I take a shaky step off. My second step is awkward, and I shoot an arm out to balance myself.

Let's hope my talk with Mama goes more smoothly.

I find her in the living room watching *Today at the Krügers*. I settle next to her on the couch, and she immediately pulls me into her side.

She says, "This is the one where the neighbor gets really nosy when the sailor visits."

I nod, remembering that episode, and begin to tap a finger against my knee. *Just talk to her*, I tell myself, and I say, "Mama, you mentioned someone named Brigitte earlier. Who is that?"

Mama startles. Her head still faces the television, but her gaze has fallen to the beige-colored carpet.

"Mama, please," I press.

"How will knowing change anything?"

"Mama, how can I answer that question without knowing all the variables?"

Mama clucks, thinking. "All the variables, huh?"

"I have gray eyes," I say.

A few beats of silence stretch between us.

"You get them from your father," Mama says finally. "Your aunt Brigitte and your grandfather have the gene for blue eyes, too. Their blues are vibrant."

My mouth falls open. I'm shocked she answered me. And now my brain is on overload: father, Aunt Brigitte, grandfather. Mama just dropped so many variables on me.

She smiles. "Where do we begin?"

It comes at almost a whisper: "My father."

"Okay," Mama says. "Okay. But first . . ." Mama motions to the kitchen sink. She mouths, *Turn it on.*

To drown out what she wants to tell me.

CHAPTER 8

I run to the sink, nearly tripping over my feet. The whooshing sound of water is added to the noise from the television. On my way back, Mama motions for me to turn the dial to the right on the television, too.

Apparently we need *a lot* of background noise to cover up what Mama wants to say. Who on earth was my father?

Mama takes my hands when I rejoin her on the couch.

"So your father," she says.

"My father," I repeat, then promptly hold my breath.

"Your father isn't with us anymore. I feel as if I should say it straightaway."

I let my breath out slowly, shakily. "I was afraid of that."

"He'd be here if he could, though, darling." Mama

squeezes my hands, and I nod, relieved. I've often wondered why it was only Mama and me.

I have to know. "What happened to him?"

"His name was Wolfgang." Mama smiles just saying his name.

I smile, thinking: *Angelika + Wolfgang = Sophie.*

Half of my equation is no longer missing. It's not missing a name anyway. "Tell me everything you know about him?"

Mama laughs softly. "Your father and I first met in 1953 here in Berlin. At a protest, actually."

I question, "A protest?"

I've never seen one here. People don't speak out like that. It's too risky. An unmarked delivery van could come for you.

Mama nods. "Back then, East Germany was becoming wholly Communist. Something called collectivization was being enforced, where things like family-owned farms became government owned."

"Like how it is now?"

"Yes. And, coupled with other changes, this collectivization left a lot of people without food. There were other reasons people were unhappy with the government, too, working conditions being one. That summer, construction workers called for a strike. Then protests began. At the one where I met your father, he was arrested, but fortunately he was released. Afterward, we stayed close, and when the United States rolled out a food relief program for East Germany, we became involved with that together. He had the biggest heart of anyone I've ever encountered. It wasn't long before we married." Mama sighs. "Mr. and Mrs. Wetzel."

Wait.

"Wetzel?" I ask. "But our last name is Ziegel."

"I'll get to that," Mama says, her smile slipping. "Your father and I lived in West Berlin. There were no walls then and we were able to come and go from one side of Berlin to the other, but even then it was becoming more difficult. Your father made it his mission to help people who wanted to leave the East find jobs and houses over in the West. After the war and before the walls went up, *millions* of people left East Germany— not all because of your father's efforts, of course, but he helped so many families. The number of refugees was incredibly embarrassing for the East. There was talk of building the Wall for a long, long time before it actually happened. Well, your father heard rumblings that it was going to happen—and soon. There were a few families he was close to getting out of the East and he insisted that he had to warn them. I was pregnant with you. Very pregnant. I didn't want him to go to the East. We argued."

Mama's eyes fill with tears. A teardrop streaks down her cheek.

"I'm sorry," I say. I'm the reason Mama's emotions are bubbling to the surface now. I put pressure on her to talk about this.

"I'm the one that should be sorry, darling. I'm the one who put off talking about this all the times you've asked. I'm the reason we're trapped here. See, I went after your father. It was the twelfth of August. I went to the home of the couple he was helping. Outside, I watched as your father was arrested. I don't know how they knew what he was up to—I *still* don't know how—but I know they took him. It was very emotional for me to watch, and it sent me into labor with you. If I'd been thinking soundly, I'd have insisted on a hospital in the West, but I wasn't thinking. I was grief-stricken and afraid, and before I knew it, I was in a hospital bed in the East. By the morning, you were born."

"The day the first wall went up," I say.

Mama nods. "Yes. I immediately asked to leave the

East. But no one was being allowed across. No one. Then, when the nurse asked my name, I couldn't give *Wetzel*. I was too afraid they'd link us to your father, and I'd go to prison and you'd be taken away from me. I gave the name Ziegel. I can't even remember where the name came from. After we left the hospital, I tracked down one of your father's friends to *become* the Ziegels. New identity. New job. New home. New everything."

"But what about my father? You said he was arrested, what if—"

"Later, that same friend told me your father died in prison."

My eyes fill with tears, too. Mama presses her forehead to mine. "I'm so sorry, Soph. I'm so sorry this is your life because of me. You could be growing up in the West. You could be anything you want to be."

"I could have an aunt and a cousin."

"What?" Mama pulls her forehead away from mine.

"I could have an aunt and a cousin," I repeat, this time louder. "Mama, this Aunt Brigitte . . . does she have a daughter my same age? Were you pregnant at the same time?"

Mama shakes her head, confused. "Where is this coming from?"

"I saw a girl the other day." I'm nervous to reveal this to Mama, as if I've done something wrong. But I haven't. "I saw a girl who looks just like me. She was on a school trip from the West."

"Did you talk to her?" Mama is quick to ask.

"There wasn't time. But, Mama, who is she? Is she really my cousin? Do we really have family on the other side of the Wall?"

Mama licks her lips, a habit we both do when we're nervous. "We should turn the faucet off. It'll seem strange if we have it running too long."

"No," I say. I rip my hands out of hers. "This conversation can't be over. How can you *continue* to keep this from me? It's bad enough you refused to tell me about my father until now. And that my last name is, what . . . made up?" I blow out air, annoyance beginning to overtake the sympathy I felt for Mama. "You're the one who is *so sorry* I don't have the life in the West I could've had, when we have family there who could take us in. *That* is the reason you always gave me, for why we couldn't ever try to escape. But they're there."

"I'm in a wheelchair, Sophie."

"Not for the first seven years of my life. Why didn't we escape then?"

"It's not that easy. You don't just snap your fingers and escape. Tell me the last time you've heard of someone even trying?"

"Hanna from school. Her brother tried."

"And when was that? A year ago? Almost two years ago? Escaping isn't an item on a to-do list. It's dangerous, Sophie, and the chances are against you. That boy got caught. His life is ruined. His family's life is ruined."

"At least he tried."

Mama shakes her head. "He didn't try well enough."

I insist, "There are other ways."

"Maybe in the beginning, when the walls were being built. But it's too difficult now. Tunnels aren't even an option anymore. Did you know the Stasi have dug their own tunnels? They run parallel with the Wall. Anyone who tries to dig out will dig straight into theirs."

But I'm not fully listening, not when I already know it's nearly impossible to escape, and not when my mind is stuck on something else I've realized. "People from the West were allowed to come for Christmas last year. They came for Easter. That girl I saw came for a school trip. People from the West can come *here* now." I all but scream, "If we can't get out, how many family members have you been keeping from coming in, Mama?"

She shushes me. It only makes me angrier.

"I thought knowing about our family would make it harder for you. Not being able to see them when you wanted. Not having the life that they have. The disappointment when there's a date planned for them to visit, but our government decides to refuse them entry. You'd only be disappointed time and time again."

"It's *you* who is disappointing me."

"That's not fair, Sophie."

"That girl . . . my *cousin*," I emphasize. "She looked shocked to see me, as if she didn't know I existed."

Mama swallows. "After the walls went up, I never contacted our family again. You have to understand that during the war I had to hide the fact I had polio. My limp could've put my father and my sister at great risk. Adolf Hitler wanted to eliminate people like me. My father was in prison for a long time because of me. And I knew that if I found a way to contact my father or sister after the Wall went up, they would've done everything within their power to rescue us. I wasn't going to put them in that type of danger again. I wasn't going to put *you* in danger again."

Some of my anger fades but not enough for me to stop from barking at her, "So instead you lied to me for my entire life? About everything?"

With that, I storm toward my bedroom, slamming the faucet off as I go.

CHAPTER 9

The fact I refused to leave my room for dinner last night means I wake with a growling tummy. But I'm still not ready to see Mama. I roll over in bed. Something crinkles beneath my face.

A piece of paper.

I turn onto my back, taking the paper with me.

There's a drawing of a tree on it.

OUR FAMILY TREE it says at the top.

I glance at my doorway. Did Mama draw this? On the tree's trunk, my name is written in what looks like Mama's handwriting. My gaze travels up toward the branches. *Wolfgang. Angelika.*

I sit up then, crisscrossing my legs beneath my blanket. I put the paper on my bed and run a finger over my father's name. His name is connected to *Wilhelm* and *Hildegard.* My grandparents. I notice that all three have *(D)* next to their names. Could it be because they are all deceased?

A pang of sadness settles in my belly.

I run my finger over to Mama's side of the tree. Above Mama is *Erich* and *Annett*. There's another of those horrible *(D)*s next to my grandmother's name. But not next to my grandfather's. The fact I have a grandparent is exciting. I wonder if he does silly things, like collect stamps or baseball cards. Mama has drawn an arrow from his name leading to a note: *Your grandpa used to be a professor of biology. (Science must run in the family.) His hobby is botany. He calls me his petunia. I've always imagined him calling you his bluestar.*

I smile at this. It appears my grandpa may collect plants, not stamps or cards.

Next to Mama's name is *Brigitte*. Her sister. My aunt. Her note says: *Your aunt Brigitte is a lot younger than me (six years). Last I knew, she worked part-time at an animal hospital. You remind me of her every day.*

I see my aunt is married to a man named Rolf. I have three cousins.

Three!

My smile grows.

Annett (16)

Erika (14)

Ava (12)

A note next to Ava says: *This is likely who you saw. Erika and Annett favor your uncle Rolf in their appearances. Ava was only a month old when the walls went up, but it was already clear she was taking after your grandma Annett. You do, too.*

I take after my grandma Annett.

The girl on the street has a name. *Ava.*

I close my eyes and let this all sink in.

"I know it's a lot," I hear Mama say.

I open my eyes, and she's leaning against the doorframe. The first thing I say is "Where is your wheelchair?"

"I'm fine for another minute or two. I hope this means you forgive me."

I study my family tree again. "It's a start. Thank you for their names. I can't believe I have three cousins," I say excitedly. But just as quickly as that excitement grows, it dims—because I have three cousins I cannot be with. Part of me understands now why Mama kept their existence from me.

But what if I could change that? What if I was able to get in contact with Ava or one of my other cousins somehow? What if they began to visit here? Another question forms, a really scary one that I've only ever allowed myself to dream about. What if my family doesn't come to us, but we go to them—for good?

I have to tell Katarina.

Her head is going to explode. Figuratively.

I tell Mama where I'm going, then rush out of the apartment. As I reach the stairs, I hear footsteps behind me. I whip around, relieved to see Monika but immediately uncomfortable that it's Monika.

She laughs. "Sorry, Soph, didn't mean to scare you. I'm running late to meet with some new friends."

I'm not sure how to act around her now. I say the first thing that comes to mind: "I'm going over to Katarina's."

"Have fun!" She passes me to bound down the stairs.

"You too!" I say, with probably too much enthusiasm.

"Oh!" Monika throws over her shoulder. "Okay if I come over in the morning? Don't leave for school until I get there."

"Why?" I'm quick to ask, but she's already rushed off without listening for my response. What is she up to? Please don't let it be anything Herr Becker won't like. I shake out my arms, hoping my nervousness goes with it.

I head out more slowly to Katarina's building down the street. At her apartment, she greets me with a "What is it? You look like you ate handfuls of mocha beans and you're a mixture of *about to be sick* and *enough energy to run a marathon*."

That about sums it up. "As if I could ever get my hands on that much mocha."

"But over in the West . . ." Katarina whispers.

I whisper back, "Funny you say that," and I step inside Katarina's apartment, closing the door. I'll worry about Monika later. "Anyone home?"

She raises an eyebrow. "No, my parents are out somewhere with my little brother."

"Great." I lead the way to her bedroom. Once inside, I turn on her hand-me-down radio for the noise of it, and I pull out my family tree from my pocket. I lay it on Katarina's bed. "There's six of them. Three cousins. An aunt. An uncle. And a grandfather."

"Slow down," Katarina says, but I can hear the

excitement in her voice. She first asks, "What is this?" but then, "*Where* did you get this?"

"My mama drew it for me. We got in a fight last night, and this morning I woke up with this on my pillow."

"Lucky. After fights with my mama, all I get is being called late to breakfast and cold potato pancakes."

I jokingly lay a sympathetic hand on her shoulder. She smiles and says, "So three cousins." Katarina taps the note Mama wrote about Ava. "And your mama thinks Ava is the one we saw, huh?"

"Yes, and now we have to figure out a way to see her again."

"When she saw you, she looked like she'd seen a ghost. Do you think she'll try to come back?"

"I hope so. But, Katy, I have another thought." I pause. I know I'm getting ahead of myself, but I also don't feel like *myself*. There's more to me than I ever realized.

"Tell me," Katarina says, "before you burst."

"I don't want to just see Ava and my family on holidays. I want to see them so much that I'm sick of them."

"Like my brother."

I point. "Exactly. And now that we know I have family on the other side to help us, what if we do more than imagine silly ways to get across? What if we figure out an actual way?"

Katarina reaches out. She touches my forehead.

I swat her hand away. "I'm not fevered. I'm serious."

We're sitting across from each other on Katarina's bed. She stares at me unblinking. "You can't be."

I shake my head.

"So you're really serious?"

I nod.

"Like seriously serious?"

"Yup."

Her eyes go wide. "But what about Hanna from school? She didn't even try to escape and things are bad for her. Imagine how bad they are for her brother and parents."

For a heartbeat, I almost take back everything I've just said. But then I remember who I'm named after. I remember my mama helped a resistance group. My aunt did, too. My father sacrificed himself to help others.

"I've got to try, Katy. I'm *going* to try to find a way to get over there."

"Wow." Katarina throws her body backward onto her pillow. Then she does a sit-up back to me. "Wow. Who are you?"

I snort. "You've got to try, too. What if you're assigned a job you don't want? Monika has been assigned a job as a pharmacist."

"What?" Katarina says, also knowing that Monika had her heart set on being a teacher.

I can only shake my head. "That could be us someday. Don't you want the life that being over on the West can give—"

Katarina holds up a hand. "You know I want it, Soph. I won't be able stop thinking about Monika and how for the next fifty years she'll be forced to do something she hates." Her voice drops further. "I think my parents hate it here, too. I overheard my mama tell my papa the other night that she feels like we're existing but not fully living. But we can't tell them or anyone about this. Not yet. We need everything figured out. All of it. Every last bit of how this is going to work or else my parents won't listen to a word I say."

"You're right." There's no way I can tell Mama either. She made it clear last night she hasn't contacted our family in order to keep them safe. To keep me safe. She will *not* be happy with me trying to find them on my own. But she'll be less angry with me if I present to her a logical and workable way to escape. The consequences of messing up this time could mean our lives and the lives of our families.

I have *so many* butterflies in my stomach. But I focus on something concrete. "First step of the scientific method is to ask a question, right?"

"Right," Katarina says, "But which question? We have two. First: How do we find Ava again to help us?"

I finish, "And how do we get across both walls?"

"This feels like a lot," Katarina says.

"It does," I say. It really does.

"But we're going to try?"

I nod. "Hard. Like really, really hard. Harder than we did with the pulley or that go-cart."

Mama said Hanna's brother *didn't try well enough.*

So we'll just have to try better.

CHAPTER 10

"Step two," I say to Katarina, beginning to pace across her small bedroom. "Background research."

To find Ava, we both agree my family tree counts as a great start to this research.

"If only your mama included last names," Katarina says, tapping Uncle Rolf's name. "Then we could have the telephone operator connect us. Boom. Simple."

Not so *Boom. Simple.* if the Stasi listen in. They can do that.

I sigh. I bet Mama purposefully didn't include last names.

"Tell me again what was in that secret hidey-hole?" Katarina asks.

I tick off what I found: "The photograph of my mama and papa. The newsprint about Sophie Scholl. A ticket stub. A receipt." I think on it. "I'm going to make an educated guess, but with the way everything was folded together, it's like my mama emptied her wallet and hid it all."

Did she do this after she got our new identity? Did she put everything she had of her old life, receipts and all, into the cavity?

Katarina asks, "What else are you thinking?"

"The receipt is probably from wherever my mama and papa lived in the West. But I don't see how having the neighborhood helps us if (a) we can't go there and poke around and (b) we don't know the last names of any of my family members. It makes it harder, too, that my mama changed our last name."

"She did what?" Katarina says.

I fill her in.

Katarina's mouth is left hanging open. "So your papa was like a secret agent, your mama once helped a resistance group, and *you* were named after a war hero. Soph, if anyone can get us over the walls, it's going to be you."

These same thoughts bolstered me to ask Mama questions and eventually decide to escape. But now that we're actually doing this, I don't feel very confident about getting us over those walls. Not one bit. "Let's move on to step three and create a hypothesis for how we can find Ava again."

I hope Katarina has an idea. She taps her bottom lip. I keep pacing. I could probably search and search all over West Berlin and never find Ava in a city so big. But what if we stand still. "Katy, what if Ava *does* try to find me again? Maybe she'll go back to where she saw me. I say we stake out the theater." It's like when I was little, Mama said if I ever got separated from her to not move a muscle. She said to stay where I was, and she'd go back to the last place she saw me.

"An excellent hypothesis, Sophie," Katarina says in a voice that mimics our teacher's. "If we wait at the theater, Ava will come to us."

"Now," I say, smiling, "let's test it."

More than anything, it's my patience that's being tested. We've been sitting on the cement steps outside the theater for ages.

I'd be surprised if Ava comes today. For many families, Sundays mean preparing a big family meal. Mama doesn't make a big fuss out of our dinners, though, with it only being the two of us. But there's six of them. That's enough to fill every seat at a large table. Maybe soon they'll need two more chairs and maybe even a second table—if Ava proves our hypothesis correct. Sadly, I don't think that'll happen today.

"It's getting late," I say to Katarina. "Should we come back after school tomorrow?"

"Won't Monika be expecting you?"

"Oh," I begin. "Monika won't be watching me after school anymore. She has training for her new job."

"Horrible," Katarina utters.

"Yeah," I say flatly. The mention of Monika reminds me she wants to come by tomorrow morning. It also makes me realize that I only have four more days until my meeting with Herr Becker. He hasn't contacted me yet, though, to tell me where and when. Maybe he won't. A girl can desperately hope.

"Sophie, we can't let what happened to Monika happen to us. We need to be scientists. It's who we are."

I know she means: *We can't get assigned jobs we don't want.*

But what I think is: *We can't get arrested and questioned by the Stasi.*

I haven't told Katarina about that other stuff yet. Or how I'm supposed to be spying on Monika. I wish I could confide in Katarina, but if I do and if Herr Becker finds out, then Mama will pay the price.

I will never let that happen. Determined, I say,

"Okay, so how are we getting over the Wall? We're on step two there. Research. What do we know? My mama says the ways people used to cross can't work anymore. But what are they? It's important to know the past, right?"

Katarina stands from the theater's steps, brushing off the back of her pants. I do the same.

As we begin to walk toward home, there's no one else out on this street. Still, my gaze darts all over, making sure there's no one who can overhear us.

"Tunnels," Katarina says. "There have been dozens of tunnels."

"Apparently, the Stasi have their own tunnels now to intercept any escape tunnels."

"Terrifying."

"There was that man who saw a gap in the Wall and derailed a train through it."

"No gaps anymore," Katarina says.

"Nope."

She says, "My favorite is still the trapeze artist on the tightrope."

"Except all the power lines from the East to the West are gone," I say. "Besides, we know my mama could never make it that way."

"Let's be serious. *I* could never make it that way either. You've seen me in phys ed class."

I certainly have. I go on, "We don't have a car to blow through a checkpoint."

"Nor do we have a tank, like that guard who crashed through the concrete."

I laugh. "Could you imagine if we didn't have a car, but we had a tank?"

"A boat could help. There was that man who swam, but didn't it take him four hours?"

I say, "I think they'd notice a boat."

"So what won't they notice?" Katarina asks. "What hasn't been done before?"

This feels daunting. Too daunting. "That's what we need to figure out, I guess."

But in the meantime, we've reached our homes.

Tomorrow Monika wants to come by. After school, we'll return to the theater and hope for Ava. We'll continue to scheme an escape. It'll be another day closer to Herr Becker. When did life get so complicated?

In the morning, I wring my hands, waiting for Monika. I have no clue what she wants to talk about. I have no clue if I *want* to know. The clock ticks and ticks. Soon, I'll be late for school.

Mama says as much.

"But Monika said she was going to stop by."

She told me not to go to school until she got here.

"I don't see her, darling. You better get going."

I pause outside Monika's door. I hear her mama singing inside, probably while she makes breakfast. But I don't hear Monika's voice. I don't see her on the staircase.

I begin to worry. Did she step out of line again? Has she been arrested a second time?

My stomach feels like I've mixed together baking soda and vinegar by the time I reach school. I slog through the school day. Not even our review of trajectory my favorite topic—can put me in a better mood.

It doesn't help that Ava doesn't come to the theater. As we wait, Katarina and I continue to brainstorm about how to get over the Wall.

"Time travel," she jokes. "We'll manipulate matter and the geometry of space-time. Your papa will get my family set up in the West well before the Wall. Then he won't go back to the East again. Your mama won't come here that night you were born. We'll both be born over there. You'll have your family. We'll still become best friends, of course."

My papa will still be alive, I think sadly to myself.

If only.

"Sophie?" Katarina says. "You're not laughing."

"Sorry, a lot on my mind. I think I'm going to go home. Same time, same place tomorrow?"

She wraps an arm around my shoulder. "Tomorrow will be the day."

I sure hope so.

We part ways outside Katarina's apartment. At my door, my key sticks in the lock. I groan and bang a fist on the door. I plan to collapse into bed and take a nap before Mama gets home. Homework can wait. *Everything* can wait.

"Come on," I grumble to my key.

But then something weird happens. The doorknob begins to move on its own—from the inside.

"Monika?" I ask. "Is that you? Did you say *after* school and not before?"

But no, I distinctly remember her saying *before*.

"Sorry to disappoint," I hear a deep voice say. The door is swung open. A man stands there. "It's only me. Welcome home, Fräulein Ziegel."

CHAPTER 11

At the sight of Herr Becker, I stumble backward.

I go all the way to the opposite hallway wall.

"You were expecting Monika, I see."

Palm pressed against the wall behind me, I'm unable to move a muscle. I certainly wasn't expecting *him*. Three days earlier than expected. *Inside* my apartment.

I've never before felt so scared and so angry.

I manage to question, "What are you doing here?"

His face is like stone. "Please, Fräulein Ziegel, won't you come in?"

Never before has the use of *please* seemed so fraudulent. Herr Becker is taller than I remembered. There's no mustache today. He's in a suit. His shoes shine.

"Let me rephrase. Come in, Sophie. Now."

My feet must move on their own because before I know it I'm walking past him into my living room. My eyes dart around, as if I'm expecting other surprises.

Everything is the same. It's mine, the apartment I've lived in my whole life. Yet everything seems unfamiliar with Herr Becker here.

The door clicks closed. I startle. Did Mama somehow let him in? I don't see her. But maybe she's in the kitchen.

"I've made coffee," he says.

He made it? I glance toward the kitchen. Mama can't be in there, then. How did he get in here? And he made coffee? I'm surprised we have any. We rarely do, with how it's in short supply in the East. But even when we do have it, Mama doesn't let me drink it. Not that it matters. What matters is he is here. In my apartment. And I'm alone with him.

"I won't tell if you have a cup," he says. "No? Very well." He gestures to the couch. "Why don't we sit down and talk? I'm sure you have much to tell me."

"I don't." But I sink down, my butt sliding down the armrest onto the couch.

"Yet you were expecting Monika just now?"

I shake my head.

He sits midway down the couch, leaving nearly half the couch open. Still, he's entirely too close. "You weren't expecting Monika? But you thought I was her. Let's not build our friendship on lies, Sophie."

"She was going to visit this morning."

"But . . ." Herr Becker eggs me on.

"She didn't?"

"Are you telling me or asking me, Sophie?"

I swallow.

"Why don't we start over?" Herr Becker says in a calm voice. "How have you been since I've seen you last, Sophie?"

I want to both laugh and cry. This man who has broken into my apartment wants to act as if we are friends? "Fine."

"Splendid. And your mother? How is she?"

"She's well," I say.

He waits, watching me. "Aren't you going to ask how I am, Sophie?"

The way he says it sends a shiver down my spine. "How are you, Herr Becker?"

"I'm glad you asked. You see, I could be better. I have many unanswered questions. Do you think you could help me with that?"

I clasp my hands together in my lap. I nod jerkily.

He smiles. "You haven't seen Monika much over the last few days, is that correct?"

His question is a relief. I'll answer. He'll see I have nothing to report. "That is correct."

"And why is that?"

"Monika said she wouldn't be watching me after school anymore because she was training at the pharmacy."

"And she seemed pleased with this new schedule?"

"Very," I lie.

Herr Becker's head tilts to one side. "Oh? So she wasn't sad about not seeing you anymore?"

"Well, she said we'd still see each other."

"Like this morning?"

"Yes."

"But you didn't see her this morning?"

"No," I say. "Is she okay?"

"Does she have cause not to be okay, Sophie?"

My breath hitches, and I want to scream. This man could win a gold medal for messing with my head. I say quickly, "No. I only found it strange she didn't come over."

"Of course." He stands and slowly walks to the kitchen. He returns with a mug. He sips. "Still hot."

Herr Becker grins, but it's the kind of smile that could freeze his steaming coffee. "I can assure you that Monika is well, currently at the pharmacy. That makes me quite happy."

Okay.

Good.

I relax a little into the couch.

"But you haven't seen her? Not at all over the past few days?"

It seems harmless enough to say, "I ran into her on the staircase yesterday."

"Is that so? And where was our Monika off to?"

"Just to meet friends."

He repeats, "Just to meet friends."

I replay my conversation with Monika through our head. "Yes, she said she was running late to meet with some new friends."

Herr Becker's eyes narrow.

What?

Did I say something wrong?

I almost ask, but I'm too afraid.

Herr Becker sips again, his eyes never leaving me. They don't even blink.

Get out, I scream in my head.

Out.

Out, out, out.

Aloud I say, "That was it. We spoke for only a second. Like I said, she was running late."

"To meet with *new* friends," he asserts. "And what about you, Sophie? Have you made any new friends lately?"

I can feel my heart pounding, and way too quickly. "No," I say.

"I suppose you don't need more friends. You and Katarina are already as thick as thieves. The two of you have spent a lot of time on those theater steps the past few days."

I stammer, "H-how do you know that?"

He only sips his stupid coffee.

"We were doing nothing wrong," I insist. "Simply sitting there."

"And talking?"

I nod and refrain from touching my face.

I know the signs of lying. Monika and I talked about them once. A change in my voice. Scratching near my mouth or eyes. My pupils getting larger. And . . . there're more signs. My brain is too frazzled to remember. I drop my gaze.

I hear Herr Becker gulp from his cup. "You've given me much to consider, Fräulein Ziegel. I thank you for that. I'll be honest that I moved forward our meeting because I wasn't entirely sure we'd be friends much longer, since Monika seemed to have fallen into line. But now I have reason to believe we may be great friends, Sophie."

He extends his empty coffee cup to me.

With shaky hands, I take it from him.

He says, "I'll see you soon."

"You don't want to go to the theater?" Katarina asks.

No.

But also *yes.* I told Herr Becker only yesterday that I was doing nothing wrong by sitting on the steps. If we don't go, will I look guilty for suddenly changing my routine?

But if Ava shows, he'll see. Or *someone* from the Stasi will see us together. I don't know who is watching me exactly. But someone is.

"You've been acting strange, Soph."

We're standing outside our school.

I don't press her on how. She caught me reading upside down again today. "Sorry," I say, "I'm just being silly. And tired. Let's go to the theater."

"Okay," she says, drawing out the word. "Fingers crossed she comes today, right?"

I nod.

Katarina takes my arm. Her head jolts toward me. "You're shaking. What's going on, Sophie? You can tell me."

I can't.

Or at least I shouldn't.

But I want to. I need Katarina's help. Everything is too much for me to do alone. I have to tell someone all that's going on. It's either Katarina or my mama.

"Sophie," Katarina presses. "What is it?"

I pop my lips, deciding to trust my best friend. But where do I begin? The beginning, I guess. I speak so softly I'm not even sure my voice can be heard. "I'm an informant."

"What?"

I lead Katarina into the street where there are no people or cars. As we cross, I say again, "I'm an informant. The Stasi contacted me that day when I went to the principal's office. Monika was arrested that morning. They asked me to spy on her after she was released."

Her mouth opens and closes like a fish's. "Monika was arrested? Is she okay? I have so many questions."

"I'll explain."

By the time I'm done, we're at the theater steps. We sit, our schoolbags at our feet. There's a chill in the air.

"You hear of people being spies all the time," Katarina says. "You never know who is and who isn't. It's wild to think you are."

"Trust me," I say, "I know. It feels like I've been carrying around bowling balls for days."

"And this Herr Becker wants to see you again?"

"*Soon*, he said. He left my apartment intrigued by something I said or something I did. It's bad enough he knows we've been coming here."

"But he doesn't know why?"

"I don't think so. Or at least he didn't let on?" I rub my brow. "Who knows."

Katarina stares at me, barely moving her mouth as she asks, "Do you think someone is watching us right now?"

I scan the street. The theater sits on a corner, with the stairs wrapping around. People are milling about in either direction. No one is taking particular notice of us halfway up the steps. No one is close enough to hear us talking, at least. "I don't know. But we should act like there is."

Katarina gasps. She tries to hide it behind her hand.

I freeze, trying not to react when all I want to do is whip my head around so I can see what she's seeing.

Behind her hand she says, "Over there."

"What?" I ask from between my teeth. "Do you think you see the Stasi?"

I'm not sure how she'd even know. They dress in everyday clothing to blend in. It's not like they wear a blinking sign that identifies them as the secret police.

Katrina whispers, "No. Not them."

I move only my eyes, trying to look in the direction Katarina is looking. I can't see far enough.

"Tell me," I say.

"It's Ava. She's here. But she's not alone."

CHAPTER 12

"Who is she with?" I ask.

I slowly turn my head, while Katarina looks in the opposite direction. I know she's going for casual, so we're not both looking the same way. I hope anyone watching believes us to be acting normal, too.

And yes, it is Ava. I can see the freckles on her face from here. We have the same long arms and legs, too, something I hadn't noticed before when we were practically nose to nose. She's right there. My pulse begins pounding excitedly.

The woman with Ava appears to be between my age and Mama's. She has blonde hair. Tall like Ava and me. If I have to guess . . . I whisper to Katarina, answering my own question, "That has to be my aunt Brigitte."

Katarina slowly faces straight again. "We've proven our hypothesis, I suppose."

We have. Ava came to find us in the very place she first saw us.

Katarina asks, "So, what do we do? This is what we've been waiting for, right?"

Right.

But I didn't expect the Stasi to also be waiting for this moment. We can't approach Ava and my aunt with the Stasi watching us. It'll be easy enough for them to track my family to the West, which will make the Stasi curious about why we were interacting with them. We'll be traitors. That would be bad. Very bad.

"I don't know what to do," I respond to Katarina. But my pulse quickens even more because I can't let this moment pass us by. I also can't let Ava come to me.

I beg my brain to come up with something.

Ava and my aunt are getting closer to the steps. My aunt's purse swings rhythmically with her footfalls. Curiously, though, Ava isn't looking in my direction. She's pointing and motioning ahead, toward the theater's entrance. Does she not want my aunt to know about me? But then why is my aunt with her? It must be because she's not allowed in the East alone. That's not surprising. But why does she want to keep me a secret?

They disappear inside the theater.

Think, I tell myself.

"Was she carrying anything?" I ask Katarina. "Did you notice a note in her hand or anything?"

"No. Nothing. Your aunt had a purse. But your cousin had nothing with her."

I nod along. "What if we write a note, then? We can leave it here on the steps."

Even as I suggest it, it sounds risky. What if Ava isn't the one to find the note? What if the Stasi get it instead? Or what if someone—*anyone*—sees me leaving a note there. That would look suspicious. There's too many ways for me to not do this well enough.

"We have to try," Katarina agrees. "But what will we say?"

Think, I demand of myself again. What should I say? How do you start a conversation that should've begun twelve years ago? I need to think of a way to keep her in the East until I can talk to her. Once she leaves, I don't know when—or if—I'll see her again.

"What if I write a restaurant and a time for later today? I'll go to the restroom and hope she follows."

Ava and my aunt emerge from the theater. Ava's hands aren't empty anymore. She's carrying a bag.

"Yes. Do it," Katarina says with urgency. "We're running out of time."

I fumble in my schoolbag for a loose leaf of paper and ask, "But where?"

"Sophie! Anywhere. Just write any restaurant name. The café down the street?"

I nod.

I write.

I fold the letter into a neat square.

"I'll shield you," she says, "the best I can from anyone behind us. Just make sure she sees you put it down."

Inside, I'm screaming. From nerves. From excitement. From fear.

I stare at Ava, willing her to make eye contact. She's a ball's throw away. A toss, really.

She meets my eye!

I wiggle the note discreetly in my hand, then leave it beside me on the steps.

Abruptly, I push Katarina to her feet. Quickly, we begin hopping down the stairs.

"Relax," Katarina says between her teeth. "Take a breath, Soph."

I do.

And again.

"Is she going for it?" I ask. Did I actually pull this off?

"I don't know," Katarina says. "I don't want to turn around."

Me either.

"What time did you write?"

"An hour."

She tucks her arm in mine. We round a corner away from the theater, away from my cousin and aunt, and away from any Stasi who may've been watching us. Did they see me leave the note? If they did, will they ambush us now? Or will they sit in wait and contact me when I least expect it? Will I find an unmarked van outside my apartment building in the morning? I will myself to stop thinking this way. Because right now I have an hour before I become an even greater traitor to East Germany. In an hour, I'll ask Ava to help us escape. That is, if she got my note.

CHAPTER 13

Not knowing if Ava is going to meet us is torture.

"She got it," Katarina assures me. "I'm sure of it."

"How can you be so sure?"

"Okay, I'm not sure. But she came back to the East. Do you think she'd go through all that effort and then not pick up a little piece of paper?"

I exhale. "True. How much longer?"

"Five minutes."

We've already circled a park, walked to the canal, glared at the Wall, and have now gone up and down the street where the café is located twice. If we do it a third time, we'll appear suspicious.

I'm so tired of living in a world where anything I do can bring suspicion upon me—and also my mama. She's the one who will suffer for my actions. Jail. An institution. Maybe the same fate as my papa. My eyes prick with emotion, and I shake my head, clearing my thoughts. I need to focus on Ava.

Katarina elbows me. "Here she comes."

My aunt is with her. Ava gestures toward the café. My aunt smiles.

I let out another slow breath. "Part of me worried my aunt wouldn't say yes to the café."

"Ava got her here," Katarina says with a smirk. "She's resourceful. I like her already."

I do, too.

My cousin.

It'll take a while for that to fully sink in.

We wait until they are seated inside, and then we approach the café.

"Wait," I say. "What if the Stasi are inside? What if they know?"

"Ava got your note or she wouldn't be here. That means the Stasi couldn't have gotten it."

"You're right."

Besides, even if they were inside, how would I tell them apart from any normal person?

I take a fortifying breath and pull open the door. A bell jingles. We go to the closest two-person table.

You have to go up to the counter to order.

"Can you get me a slice of the krusta? Something small."

"Wouldn't want to spoil your dinner." Katarina smiles.

But I know that smile is actually because while she's ordering, I'll be meeting with my cousin in the restroom.

Good luck, she mouths.

I wipe my palms down my pant legs. I have to appear normal. No normal person would be overly excited to use a public restroom. I push open the door, letting it fully shut behind me, and promptly check each stall to make sure I'm the only one in here.

I go to the sink, holding on with both hands to steady myself. I look in the mirror. My cheeks are rosy.

The bathroom door opens, and Ava comes in.

"Hello," she says.

"Ava?" Part of me is shocked my plan worked.

She nods, a smile already stretched across her face. "So it's true, you're Aunt Angelika's daughter?" She lets out a sound that's a mix between disbelief and astonishment. "I can't believe it. I'm sorry, I don't even know your name. No one does."

I rush to turn on the sink's faucet. I should've done it right away.

Ava cocks her head at me, but then she nods. "Our grandpa says our mamas grew up in a time of *eyes and ears*. It's like that here, too, isn't it?"

"Yes."

"I'm sorry. That's horrible. It always feels different when I'm here. Like I need to be on my best behavior."

"Yet here you are sneaking into bathrooms to talk to me . . . I'm Sophie."

"Sophie," she repeats. Then Ava's arms are around me. She pulls back. She looks at me. "Like Sophie Scholl? Wow. I've heard all the stories. I still can't believe this. When I saw you . . ." She shakes her head, as if there aren't words. "We've been looking for you. Well, for Aunt Angelika. We thought you'd be hard to recognize. Joke's on me. Look at us." We both turn to face the mirror. Same freckles. Same eyes. Same hair, except for hers being blonde and mine brown. "We're even the same height. Imagine if I never found you? Like I said, my mama's been looking. She comes over here as much as she's allowed without raising suspicion. There's a limit, and she gets denied sometimes. When she can, though, she walks around to look for your mama." Ava pauses for a gulp of air. "Then I was over here for my school trip. And I saw you. I couldn't believe it. I've told no one. I was afraid I was wrong. After I saw you, though, I purposely left my schoolbag at the theater. I needed an excuse to come back. My mama always told me if I got lost, that I should stay where I was, and she'd go back to the last place we were together." Just like Mama. "I hoped you'd do the same. And you did. This is unbelievable. Here you are. You do exist. Everyone is going to go nuts when I tell them. Oh my god. I'll shut up now. You say something."

"Something."

She laughs.

I laugh.

"I saw you ordered the krusta. I got it, too. Is that your version of pizza?"

"Pizza?"

She smiles. "Now, that's insulting to food, not to know what pizza is."

And while I want to continue to be silly like this—*like cousins*—I know our time is ticking. "Ava, we only have a minute or two." We both glance at the door, knowing someone could come in at any moment. Surely they'll think it's odd that two girls are standing at a sink that's gushing water and no one is washing their hands. "I'll just say it. We want to escape. Well, me and my friend Katarina are the ones scheming. My mama doesn't know anything about it yet. But Mama always said we couldn't escape because we don't have family in the West to help us."

Ava's brows scrunch in confusion. "She's never told you about us? Any of us?"

I shake my head. "Not until after I saw you. That's not important right now. I mean, it is. But right now we need to figure out a way to see each other again so we can keep planning. I still don't know how we'll get across. My mama's in a wheelchair, too. That won't make it any easier."

"Her polio? My mama told me there was a chance it could come back."

"Yes."

It hurts to think that Ava knows so much about us. She instantly knew who I was named after. She knew about Mama's polio. Yet, I didn't even know she existed until days ago. I swallow down the lump in my throat and go on. "Once I figure out a way to cross, I'll need your help."

"Of course. Anything."

Despite how serious this conversation is, a smile still creeps onto my face. I have family who'll help.

She suggests, "Give me your address. I'll give you mine."

"All right," I say. "But we need to be careful what we say. They read our mail here."

"I've heard that," she says. "Oh, Sophie, we'll get you out of here."

That *we* is both encouraging but also makes me cross and rub my arms. What if Ava does everything right but I do it all wrong? Mama has protected them all these years. What if I undo all of it by including them in my planning?

Ava squeezes my hand. "We will, Sophie. You're getting out of here. You have to."

CHAPTER 14

A few days later, a letter arrives addressed to me. I usually get the mail, but I'm especially glad I did today. Finding Ava was a ginormous step forward, but I still haven't told Mama anything. And boy, do I feel guilty I haven't told her I met with Ava or that I've seen her sister with my own two eyes. Ava and I agreed the café wasn't the right place to meet my aunt Brigitte, but I know my aunt knows about me now.

It has been weighing on me. Mama's even asked me if something was wrong. Then asked if I had any more questions about our family.

The fact I said no probably raised her eyebrows. But I covered by saying I was worried about not seeing Monika again. Mama only smiled and told me that Monika is an adult now with adult responsibilities.

I begin to tear the envelope open, shocked that Ava has written me so quickly after we met, as I walk to my bedroom. I close the door, just in case Mama returns home early. What will Ava say? Will she ask me if I have any ideas? *How* will she even word that question?

Sadly, I don't have an answer for her yet. I've been thinking. I know the ways people have crossed before: Background research is complete. It's time to construct a hypothesis, a possible method for crossing. It needs to be something new. Something ingenious. That's where I'm stumped. But I'm a scientist. I have an Inventor's Box to prove it.

But for now . . . this letter.

I remove the paper from the envelope and unfold it.

At first, I notice the lettering is block-like. Not what I expected from Ava. I look at the envelope again, realizing there's no return address. The handwriting for the address appears to have been written by someone else.

Strange.

My eyes jump to the signature at the bottom.

The offices of Herr Becker.

I drop the paper, suddenly feeling as if it could scorch my skin. It floats lazily—back and forth, back and forth—to the floor. I imagine it growing hotter. I picture it releasing smoke, and I plead that the fibers of the paper will spontaneously combust.

Poof.

Gone.

But that'll solve nothing. What he wants me to know won't disappear. I slowly kneel to the floor and pick up the paper. I'm almost surprised when it feels cool to the touch.

Dearest Sophie, it begins.

Goose bumps erupt on my skin. From Katarina, this greeting would seem silly. From Herr Becker, it feels like a trap.

It's almost time for us to meet again. Does two days' time work for you? I'd like to extend an invitation for you to come to my office.

He provides a time.

He lists an address.

And that is that.

In two days, I'll be walking straight into the lion's den.

The building looms before me.

The House of Ministries.

It's the address Herr Becker gave me. It was once the largest office building in all of Europe. Maybe it still is? I remember the building being a source of pride for East Berlin that was touted in my lessons.

The stone building stretches an entire block wide and seven stories high. There are rows and rows of windows. I've walked past it before, but I always gave the building a wide berth because—quite simply—it's the House of Ministries. I've heard that this is where many of the big names of our government have offices. Like Herr Willi Stoph, who is the equivalent of the prime minister of the German Democratic Republic.

Apparently, Herr Becker is important enough to have an office here, too.

I suck in a breath and swivel my head, feeling as if I'm being watched. The building is close to the Wall. Real close. In fact, the House of Ministries runs right along the first wall.

When the Wall first went up, many buildings were affected. Sometimes the Wall ran right into them, connecting to both sides of a building, so the front side was on the East side but the backside was on the West side.

At first, when the Wall was little more than barbed wire, people jumped out of windows to freedom. Mama told me they threw down mattresses to soften the landing. Or people on the West held nets to catch jumpers. But that type of escape didn't last long. Windows were boarded up and even filled with bricks. Some buildings were leveled.

Then the first wall was completed with concrete and a second wall was erected, the death strip between them. Even if a person somehow got through a window, they'd land in that no-man's-land of trip wires, snarling dogs, and watchtowers, where guards wait with guns.

I realize that while all these thoughts pass through my brain, I've been staring absently at the Wall and one of those guards from the watchtower *has* been staring back at me.

He motions with his gun to *get going.*

I hurry toward the entrance of the House of Ministries.

As I enter, I slow my steps, taking deep breaths, willing courage to flood my body. *Never* did I imagine going inside this building.

If anyone finds it peculiar that a twelve-year-old is walking into the lobby by herself, they don't let on. A woman even greets me in a stiff voice, asking my name, then leads me deeper into the building. It's like a maze of beige walls, and I soon lose track of where I am, which floor I'm on even.

"We're here," she says to me in a nasally voice. She knocks softly on a wooden door, waiting for a deep-toned *Enter* before she turns the knob.

"Fräulein Ziegel has arrived, sir."

"Wonderful, and right on time. Please send her in."

The woman steps aside, clearing the doorway to the room, but doesn't say a word, doesn't smile. She turns on her heel and leaves.

"Sophie," I hear. "Are you still out there?"

I step forward.

"Ah, there you are. Come in, won't you?" Herr Becker sits behind a large desk. The fakest smile I've ever seen is on his face. He gestures to a visitor chair.

I go to it. Sit down. His office is spotless and as sterile as an operating room.

"I'm so glad you got my letter. One can never be sure a piece of mail will actually get where it's going. Did you know that we have special machines that can open, copy, then reseal pieces of mail? We go through ninety thousand letters a day. Can you believe it? Any time someone sends or receives a letter, it's like a game of chance. And chances are, a file is created on that person."

He laughs and wiggles his brows, as if he told a joke.

He points. "Look at those file cabinets. Each one is stuffed with files."

I feel sick.

Is he telling me this because of his letter? Or does he know that Ava and I plan to communicate by mail? Is this a warning? But why would he warn me at all?

"We also can listen in on phone calls." Finally, not something I need to worry about. We don't have a phone. I wonder now if Mama chose purposely not to have one so it'd be harder for family to contact us, and thus be at risk. "And," Herr Becker prattles on, "we can bug apartments and homes. The devices are so small"—he pinches his fingers together until they are nearly touching—"that we hide them in the tiniest of places to record everything someone says. Isn't that cool? That is the word you young people use, correct?"

I nod, horrified by the idea of bugs being in our homes. Herr Becker could easily have placed one in mine when he was in my apartment. But why would he warn me of this either?

He looks pleased with himself, leaning back in his chair. He casually reaches to pull open a drawer. He removes a few files and drops them on the desk with a *thud*.

They're upside down to me, but thanks to my practice I easily recognize my name, my mama's name, Monika's name. Slowly, he leans forward, sitting straight again. "Sophie, I want us to be good friends. I've said this before."

Yet he broke into my home. Yet he tries to intimidate me.

He goes on, "You know, there are over sixteen million people in East Germany. And while there are many, many adults who secretly work for us, we don't approach many people your age. But you're special, Sophie. You can do so much good for us—*with* us. Already, you've been a great help."

He pauses then, as if he expects me to ask how. A small insolent part of me wants to widen my eyes at him, saying, *Well, go on, then. You love to hear yourself talk.* But I wouldn't dare do that.

"Don't you want to know how?" he asks me.

In my lap, I clench my hands together. "How?"

"It was a word. A single word. You said *new*. Monika has *new* friends. That's the reason why you and I are to remain friends. We originally had reason to believe that Monika wouldn't continue to be a problem, but that word *new* got me thinking that perhaps Monika has fallen into the wrong crowd. A crowd that undermines our rules and beliefs. Not like you. You and Katarina are good East Germans." He cocks his head. "Though I did hear you didn't go to the theater's steps the past few days. I guess you two are sick of that spot?" He waves his hand, and I fight to keep my expression stoic. "Anyway, I'd like you to keep your eyes and ears open. Let me know if you see Monika with anyone. If you can get their names, you get bonus points. Think of it like a game. I love games, you've likely noticed. How does that sound, Sophie? Will you keep an extra-close eye on Monika?"

I'm quick to tell him what he wants to hear. "Yes."

He smiles, but his brown eyes seem to darken. "Good. But remember, Sophie, all games have winners and losers. I never lose, but if I find out you're lying to me or withholding information from me, you will." He taps Mama's file. "You *both* will lose."

CHAPTER 15

"There's not a single part of me that likes that man, Soph."

Side by side, Katarina and I sit on swings at a barely usable playground. My feet drag forward, then backward. I went straight from my meeting with Herr Becker to Katarina's door. I needed my best friend. "It's like his goal in life is to intimidate me."

"He can do a lot more than that. Phone taps. Bugs." She does a full-body shiver, sending her swing off course and bumping into mine.

I plant my feet. "Which is why we need that hypothesis as to how we'll get to the other side. And fast. He's threatened me about my mama more than once, and I'm afraid that if Monika is arrested again, she won't be coming back."

"You wouldn't dare say anything to Herr Becker about her, would you?"

I dig the toe of my shoe into the dirt. "Don't look at me that way, Katy."

"Like what?"

"Like a sad puppy. I wouldn't *want* to tell on Monika. But it's either her or my mama. What would you do?"

She squeezes my hand where I grip the swing. "You won't have to decide. A hypothesis. Now. Go. We can't go under that thing." She nods in the direction of the Wall.

"We can't go through it. The only option is to go *over* it. High above it like Sophie Blanchard and Katharina Paulus."

I dip my head back. In the cloudy, dark sky, I picture the yellow-striped balloon.

Katarina says, "Our catapult idea isn't sounding as cuckoo anymore, huh?"

That gets a smile out of me, my first one of the day. "Let's collect," I suggest. "We could find something that sparks a good idea."

It's how we found better material to perfect our slingshot and improve our go-cart.

Katarina swings on my left. On my right, a broken swing is on the ground, half covered with dirt. I twist to kick it with my foot. "A seat," I say. "Mama will need to sit or be helped over in some way."

"Yes!" Katarina says with some gusto. I actually startle at her voice. We so often speak in whispers. "Pick that baby up."

I let out a snort, then dig free the swing. Rusty old chains are still attached to it.

"This is good, Soph. We're on the right path."

With a broken, rusty swing? I wish I felt as confident. But yes, it's a start.

By the end of our hunt, we've added an old leather purse with a long strap, an empty paint can, a bent handlebar from a bike, and a slew of items we'll actually recycle. Katarina takes those. I take the rest to add to my Inventor's Box. One man's junk is another girl's treasure.

In the lobby, I see the paternoster is being worked on. There's an *Out of Order* sign dancing across the compartment, and the floor of it is opened, showing nothing but darkness beneath. A long stretch of the lift's chain is stretched across the lobby. The maintenance man works with a large spool of cable, too, perhaps to help him insert and loop the chain?

With my arms full, I don't stay to watch.

In my hallway, I pass Monika's door. Then I stop. Noises. Voices. It sounds like they have people over, which they don't do very often. I wonder if it's Monika and her *new* friends. The "crowd" that Herr Becker wants me to investigate to figure out if Monika is still defying our government.

But investigating is the last thing I want to do. I tried to avoid Monika, and I *still* let slip something Herr Becker found useful.

I squeeze my eyes shut and let out a growl. Maybe it's a groan. Or both.

I have to warn Monika. Maybe it'll stop her from doing something that Herr Becker will pressure me into telling him about. Maybe it'll save me from having to pick between Mama and her.

But then I remember Herr Becker's bugs. If he so easily snuck into my apartment, could he have done the same to hers?

The voices in her apartment grow louder.

I hear, "I hate that stupid job! I won't do it. I won't!"

Monika.

No.

Stop talking!

I run to her door. It's locked. I rattle the knob while I knock. The apartment goes silent. As soon as Monika opens her door, I press a finger to my lips.

"What is it, Soph?"

I widen my eyes and tap my finger against my lips with more vigor.

Worry lines form between her brows.

Behind her, I see a handful of people around Monika's age sitting on her couch and chairs. My heart sinks. She does have a new crowd, and with the way Monika's cheeks are flushed, that outburst may not have been her first. Not only that, but she just said my name. If there is a bug, how much did it hear?

I backstep into the hallway, hoping she'll follow. Monika peers over her shoulder. "Be right back," she says, then follows me.

"Shh," I chastise.

"What gives?" she says. "Did you hear us?"

For a moment, I stare at her. This is Monika. The Monika I've known my whole life. Who is more than a babysitter—like a sister. Who brought me my first treasure and encouraged me to begin my Inventor's Box. Who patched my knees whenever I fell. Who is now knee-deep in danger. Who I also need to get over the Wall. And I will, but right now, I'm even more determined to warn her. I have to tell her about Herr Becker.

I walk farther down the hall, turning my head up and down, left and right, inspecting each painting and light fixture. Can bugs be attached anywhere? And what would the device look like, besides being tiny? I juggle the paint can, the handlebar, and the purse in my arms.

"What on earth are you doing?"

"Shh!" I say again.

I find a spot in between apartment doors where I don't think there's anywhere to hide a bug. Then I whisper, "The Stasi think you've fallen into the wrong crowd. Are those people inside your apartment the wrong crowd?"

Monika's mouth drops open. She extends her pinkie.

It's all the answer I need. With the stuff I'm holding, I awkwardly link our hands.

But then she asks me, "How do you know the Stasi are watching me still?"

I don't want to answer that.

Monika hasn't let go of our pinkie swear. She shakes our hands, urging me to respond. The handlebar clunks to the floor. "They contacted me," I confess. "Made me sign something. It's *me* who is supposed to watch you."

Monika pulls her pinkie from mine. There's hurt in her eyes. "And are you?"

"Of course not," I say in a loud whisper. "I'm trying to warn you. But he says if I lie to him—"

"If you lie to your controller . . ." she says, shaking her head in disbelief.

My *controller*. The term and what it implies makes me hate Herr Becker even more. "If I lie to him, he'll put my mama in an institution."

Monika still looks like steam could pour from her ears, but her expression also softens.

"Monika, he said they use phone taps and bugs."

Her eyes go wide. She clamps a hand over her mouth as she looks back toward her apartment.

But it's too late. If there was a bug to hear her, it already heard her shouting. Still, Monika races toward her door, no doubt to stop her new friends from saying anything else that could get them arrested.

I'm left standing in the hallway alone. One of the lights flickers. I hate this place. I hate everything about living on this side of the Wall. My eyes fill with tears, and I slowly bend to pick up the handlebar that fell. All I want to do is crawl under my covers and—

"Sophie!"

"Katy?" She's panting. "Did you run here?"

"Herr Becker . . ." She clutches onto my arm.

"What is it?" I plead.

"He called my apartment."

"What? When?"

"Just now . . ."

Our voices cross, me asking, "Why?" and Katarina saying, "He says he wants you to come to his office. Right now. Like . . . *right now*."

CHAPTER 16

Right now.

"He asked for you," Katarina emphasizes.

My *controller* asked for me through my best friend. "Because we don't have a phone," I say, feeling comatose. Staggering down the hall toward my apartment, I utter, "He called you to get to me." I plod inside, still carrying my treasures, and into my bedroom.

"Yes, Sophie. And did you not hear me?"

"I heard you," I say, and collapse to my knees in front of my Inventor's Box.

Once opened, I methodically place each of our new finds inside. The purse. The paint can. The handlebar. The last is too big. I turn it at an angle. The lid of my Inventor's Box won't close.

Katarina places a hand on my shoulder, and suddenly everything feels like too much.

Herr Becker wants to see me.

Only moments ago, I revealed myself to Monika.

Only moments before that she said my name.

Only moments before that Monika was screaming about hating her assigned job.

He must've been listening.

He instantly called Katarina.

He wants to see me now.

My Inventor's Box begins to blur. My chest is rising and falling too quickly. I can feel my heartbeat in my ears. Panic seizes me. Am I hyperventilating? My brain tells me carbon dioxide is leaving my body faster than it should.

I clutch either side of my box, then reach inside to retrieve a paper bag. I hold it over my mouth. In. Out. In. Out. I rebreathe the air trapped in the bag. I feel the heat of my breath. I imagine the CO_2 I lost from breathing too quickly going back into my body.

"You're okay, Soph," Katarina says, rubbing my back. "You're okay."

I start to feel that way again, too.

I lower the bag. "I'm okay." But I absolutely, totally, positively dread what I have to say next. "I better hurry."

Katarina says, "I'll walk you there."

We don't say a word as we make our way toward the

House of Ministries. The closer we get, the faster my feet move, as if there's a time limit for me to get there and I already wasted too much of it. I leave Katarina outside, after she assures me she won't move a muscle, and step into the lobby.

The nasally voiced woman from before isn't there. No one else approaches. I'm too afraid to keep Herr Becker waiting any longer. I continue on, no one stopping me. I'm not sure where I'm going. I remember going up to a higher floor. I do that. Each beige hallway looks like the next. I think about asking a man coming toward me for directions, but he shouts a profanity at whatever he's reading as he walks and I decide against it.

Panic begins to set in again. I should've brought my paper bag.

I turn a corner. A dead end, nothing but windows at the end of the hall.

I'm about to try a new hallway, but I stop. The scene outside the window looks different somehow. Brighter. More colorful. I step closer, my eyes trained on a red-and-white sign in the distance. It's on the side of a tall building.

Coca-Cola, I read.

But we don't have that drink here. We have Vita Cola.

We don't even have those types of signs. Like posters, but much larger. What are they called . . . billboards? There's no need for them here when the government owns everything that's for sale. There's no need for competition. But there is . . . in the West.

It couldn't be.

Could it?

Is that the West?

So close?

Confused, I run toward the windows. I'm a few floors high. Up here, I can see that there's a stretch of land below me. It stops at a wall. But then on the other side of that wall are people walking. There are cars. There are buildings, like the one with the Coca-Cola billboard.

I blink, even more confused. The wall I see must be the second, outer wall. But where is the first?

I press my cheek against the window. The coldness of the glass sparks goose bumps on my skin. My hurried breaths begin to cloud the window. And I can't believe it, farther down, where the wall bends, I see a watchtower and the first wall. That can only mean one thing: The first wall stops when it touches this portion of the House of Ministries and begins again on the other side.

And right now, I'm standing in the middle of the "death strip" but *inside* the House of Ministries. My brain begins to itch with how huge this discovery is.

"Fräulein Ziegel."

I jump at my name.

"There you are." It's the nasally voiced woman. She grumbles, "I have been looking all over for you. How dare you walk these halls alone."

"Herr Becker asked me to come," I insist.

"I very well know that. This way. Hurry. He doesn't like to be kept waiting."

I clench my teeth together as I join her. If she'd been waiting for me in the lobby, then I wouldn't have entered the building alone. On the other hand, it feels like a stroke of luck she was not there and that I stumbled upon this glimpse of the West. It feels important. It's the closest to the West I've ever been.

Too soon, the woman is knocking on Herr Becker's door and I'm in his visitor chair.

At first, he doesn't speak. He stares at me, as if expecting me to talk first. I clutch my hands together, still saying nothing. Finally, he says, "Your family should have a phone."

You contacted me easily enough, I wish I had the nerve to say. But instead I say, "My mama has never wanted one."

"Strange, don't you think?"

I respond, "There are others without phones."

"Well," Herr Becker says as he steeples his fingers, "when you return home, you'll find that a telephone has been installed within your apartment."

"There's no need for—"

But Herr Becker raises his hand for me to stop talking. "Do you know why I asked you here?"

I swallow. Lying could mean trouble for Mama. "You were listening at Monika's."

"And?"

He doesn't deny it. So he *did* bug her apartment, just as I had feared. And he heard Monika say my name. He knows I was there.

I'm careful not to touch my face, not to squirm, not to look away, not to show signs that I could be lying to him. "I went over but then I saw she had people there and I got scared and left."

"You left?"

I nod.

"Even though I explicitly asked you to figure out who those friends were? Did you hear what they were saying?"

Why is he asking me this? If he bugged her apartment, he knows what she said. "She didn't mean it."

"Mean what?" Herr Becker asks.

He wants me to say it. "She doesn't hate her job."

His head ticks. "So why did she say it?"

I open my mouth. I have no idea what to say. What can I say to make this better, not worse? "Please don't take her away again."

Against his desk, Herr Becker taps his left hand. His right hand. His left. His right. The whole time, he says nothing. He just taps. And taps. Back and forth, like he's playing the drums. Until finally: "It's up to you if I take her away or not. I need names. First names. Last names. I don't have time to sit here and listen to the prolonged prattling of teenagers. Get me those names. I assume you understand the consequences if you fail to handle this assignment."

"I understand."

Both Mama's and Monika's fates are up to me.

"Good." He pulls open a drawer. Slams it. Herr Becker storms out of his office, calling for someone and something. When he returns, he has a single card. "My office number. Call it with names. Call me if you have something important to say. Otherwise, I will see you in one week and I can glean for myself if there's any need for us to remain friends. But if not, Sophie . . . well, you're a smart girl. You know what will happen to Monika. You know what will happen to your mother."

He dismisses me.

I can't get away from his office and his threats fast enough. I find the woman waiting for me. She walks two steps ahead of me, not turning around even once to make sure I'm following. She has a zip-cord-like contraption around her waist that I can't help but admire. On it, keys dangle, emphasizing each abrupt footstep she takes.

Outside, Katarina is waiting, her arms crossed and hugging herself. "You're okay," she breathes.

"For now."

"What did he say? What did he want?"

"I'll get to that. But first I have something more important to tell you."

"More important? Sophie, what on earth could be more important?"

For now I leave her question unanswered and lead us away. Mama and Monika being in danger is huge. But Herr Becker is playing games with me. I need to be savvy enough to play them back. And right now the biggest way I can stick it to him is to disappear, taking his leverage of Mama and Monika with me. Once Katarina and I have distanced ourselves by two blocks, I whisper, "I saw the West. Like, I really saw it, more than just seeing people on those stupid platforms looking into our side."

Her eyes are huge and round. "What? How?"

"The House of Ministries is along the first wall, right? I thought it was just a simple square or rectangle. But it's not. There are portions of that building that stick out. I stood at the tip of one part that juts out *past* the first wall."

"What are you saying?"

"I was *within* the death strip but above the walls, high enough where I could see into the West. It wasn't that far. I don't know how far, for sure. I need to look again because I got interrupted. But, Katy, that is where we'll do it. *That* is where we'll escape . . . from right under Herr Becker's nose."

CHAPTER 17

We'll go over and out. That's what we'll do. We'll only need to go over one wall instead of two and only traverse half the death strip instead of all of it. That's huge. But how will we do it?

That question still remains, and I try really hard not to let my growing confidence fall through my fingers like loose dirt from the playground.

Especially, as I approach my apartment, because . . . I hear voices.

My stomach clenches until I realize it's only the television. With an exhale, I go inside. But then I suck that air right back in. There's always been a table by the door. Like always, there's mail on it. Now there's also a telephone. It's black and shiny, reminding me of a black whip snake, the kind that can uncoil and lurch in a heartbeat.

Even knowing it was going to be here, I do a double take. I'm reminded *once again* that Herr Becker likes to play games. He did this to show me how much power he has.

"Surprised me, too," Mama says, and I jump at her voice. She's in her wheelchair next to the couch.

I point at the telephone and arrange my face to appear confused: eyebrows scrunched, head tilted.

"It just happened," Mama said. "I was watching television when two men came knocking. They barely said two words . . ."

I know Mama well enough to know she's waiting for me to chime in about whether I know anything. "Oh?"

She wheels closer and pats her lap for me to sit.

"Mama, no. That's weird."

She smiles. "Come sit."

I laugh. "I'm too big. I'll crush you."

"Never." Mama stretches her arms out toward me. She wiggles her fingers. "Besides, I feel like I haven't seen you, always busy and running off."

I also know Mama tends to get her way. I sit on her lap. I feel awkward at first, but she pulls me into her. It's kind of nice.

She whispers into my ear, "I checked for bugs."

I startle away from her mouth, sitting straighter, the sudden lap sitting now making more sense.

Mama studies my reaction. Then says, "I wasn't entirely sure what I was looking for. The Stasi can listen in on any telephone call, but bugs can be added to the actual telephone receiver to pick up conversations *around* the phone, too." Mama circles her arm to include our living room. "Or at least I think that's how bugs work. All I know is that I didn't request a telephone. And even if I did, requests are generally only granted if a person is a privileged Communist Party member. Or"—Mama pauses—"if a person is considered a political dissident and the Stasi want to listen in on their conversations."

"A dissident?"

"What do you think that word means, Sophie?"

"Someone like Monika?"

"Yes." Mama is still studying me. I avert my eyes. "We keep our heads down, so while we're not *bad* Communists, I also don't think we're the type of citizens who randomly receive an unrequested telephone. Do you have any idea why we'd receive one?"

The profanity I overheard the man use in the hallway flutters through my head. I'd never dare say it out loud. In the past, I'd also never lie to Mama. But I can't tell her I'm working with Herr Becker. She'll go bonkers. She'll demand I stop, no matter that *she'll* be the one who pays the price. I search for words now that feel more like a fib instead of a lie. "Maybe because Monika is our next-door neighbor. She was arrested, right? They could be keeping an eye on her and those around her?"

"Maybe," Mama says slowly.

Never before have I felt heavier, like a sack of potatoes in my mama's lap.

"You'd tell me if something is going on with you?" She gives my chin a quick squeeze, and this time I force myself not to look away. It feels like a spider is climbing up my throat. I clear it and decide to continue down my fibbing path. "There is something I want to tell you. It only just happened. You told me about our family. About Ava. Well, Katy and I kept going back to where we saw her that first time. And, um, Ava came back."

"Did you talk to her?"

I can't tell if the urgency in Mama's voice is anger or eagerness.

I nod. "Only really quickly. We met in the bathroom."

Mama glances at the telephone. Is she wondering if my conversation with Ava put us on the Stasi's radar?

"I turned on the faucet in the restroom," I say, to try to reassure her.

"I see."

I wait for her to hurtle a zillion questions at me. She glances at the telephone again.

"Mama, I was careful, I swear—"

"Mail came for you today."

My head swivels toward the stack of mail, which is right next to the new telephone.

Mama goes on, "It's postmarked from the West, so it's making more sense now."

"Did you open it?" I ask.

"Of course not, Sophie. It's addressed to you."

I begin to climb out of her lap.

"Don't get up," she says, and gives us a push. "A benefit of being on wheels."

I can't help but laugh as we roll toward the table. In fact, I feel giddy.

A letter.

From Ava.

This time that's got to be who it's from. But just in case, I cross my fingers before I pick it up. I leave them crossed an extra breath, pleading that Ava was smart about whatever she wrote.

"My goodness. Open it already, Sophie."

We exchange a smile. I love that Mama is excited, too.

I slide my finger through the envelope's flap, wondering if the Stasi's machines have already opened and resealed it. Is there a copy of this letter in Mama's folder now? In mine?

Shaking away the thought, I pull free the letter.

I'm relieved to find the writing isn't block-like.

Expect us on Easter.

Mama and I lock eyes. Then we laugh, together.

On Easter, Mama is going to see her family for the first time in twelve years.

And on Easter, I'm going to see the rest of my family for the first time ever.

Also on Easter, Ava and I are going to finalize the plan for our escape.

I have *two weeks*.

CHAPTER 18

I never thought the day would come where I have this thought, but . . . I can't wait for my next meeting with Herr Becker. I *need* to be back in that building.

I don't *want* to tell him anything about Monika.

But I also can't meet with him without anything to say about Monika.

I'm in a pickle. A big, smelly one.

Unless . . .

I turn my head toward Monika's apartment. I'm in my bedroom, slumped against my bed's headboard. There are at least three walls between me and my friend, but I stare at my cream-colored wall as if I have X-ray vision and can see all the way through and through and through. Is Monika over there? It's a Sunday. There's no school. Mama was pulled into work today, but I doubt Monika has pharmacy training.

If she does, I bet she's crying her eyes out or

daydreaming about the next time she can meet with her new friends.

Rubbing my lips together, I formulate a plan. In the end, it's simple. Monika and I need to work together. Like any successful experiment, it needs to be carefully handled, each step calculated just so. When it comes to Herr Becker and the Stasi, there's no room for error. That's the tricky part; I need to talk to Monika without bugs hearing us or spies seeing us. Covertly. Secretly.

I sit up and straighten my spine.

Science tells us that our body can affect our thinking. Slouching can shrink how much room our lungs have, up to thirty percent. That means less oxygen to our brains. I need all the oxygen I can get right now.

I breathe deeply, imagining my brain waking up. But I'm still not getting my brain where it needs to be. My thoughts feel sluggish. I stand and begin to pace. Monika once told me we can actively change the pace of our thoughts by walking more briskly or by slowing down.

Briskly it is.

My eyes fall on my pillow, and it comes to me—how Monika and I will talk. We'll write it down. It's such a simple solution that it's almost comical I've hotfooted back and forth across my bedroom this long. We once played an anagram game where she scrambled letters within a word. After I put them in order, I revealed her secret message:

Monika is the best.

I smile at the memory. And also realize our exchange doesn't need to be this complicated. All we really need is a paper, pen, and the right words—secret ones.

Behind my back, I hold a letter—with those very secret words. I knock on Monika's door and plead over and over and over for Monika to be the one who answers.

Phooey.

"Hello, Frau Voigt. Is Monika in?"

"Sophie! How wonderful to see you. Yes, you just caught her. She's in her room getting ready for this or that. You know the way."

I smile and head inside, covertly switching my letter from behind me to in front of me as I pass Monika's mama. The last thing I want is her seeing my letter and saying anything out loud I don't want her to say. The bug could still be listening. Or can it only listen for so long? Does it have a battery that'll run out? I can't know for sure, so I need to be careful.

Fortunately, I pass unscathed and hurry toward Monika's room.

"Monika!"

My voice is higher than usual.

"Sophie?"

I rush toward her, handing her my letter.

Read, I mouth to her.

As she begins, I fill the quiet with rambling. If Herr Becker can hear us right now, he'll likely become suspicious if there are pauses in our conversation. "I thought I'd stop by and say hi. We haven't seen each other too much. I miss you."

Monika glances at me. I know what she just read: *Monika, do not read this out loud. You know I'm a spy. I need your help.*

"I miss you, too," she says, still reading.

I go on, "I had to tell you about this funny thing that happened in school."

This time, Monika does more than glance. She looks up, her eyes big, and mouths back, *That won't happen.* I'm guessing she just read *Herr Becker is expecting me to report on you. I need something to tell him or else he'll put my mama in an institution.*

I left off how Monika's in danger, too. I don't want to scare her. Besides, she'd care more about my mama than herself.

I continue my ruse, saying, "Katarina was running late to class, so she was literally running late into class. She caught someone's foot as she was rushing and went flying."

"Oh no," Monika says without looking up.

"This is the funny part. She landed right in Anton's lap like she was aiming for him."

"She did not!"

"She did!" Poor Katarina. This conversation may be staged, but the story is 100 percent real.

"Guess Katy is the one who hit the bull's-eye," Monika says, the joke a nod toward how Anton is into archery. Monika puts aside the paper and nods. She's finished reading the rest: *Tell me something I can tell him. Something that won't get you in trouble.*

"Poor Katarina," she says. "Did she turn bright red?"

"She sure did. Katy jumped up so quick it was like his lap was lava. She didn't look at him a *single* time the rest of class."

"Now, that's a first."

We both laugh.

Then Monika says, "I wish I could talk longer, but I'm actually running out to meet some friends."

"Oh?" I say. Suddenly, butterflies are banging together in my stomach. I'm nervous that if Herr Becker is somehow hearing this, Monika may say the wrong thing.

Relax, she mouths. She grabs a pen from her desk and starts writing on my letter. As she's writing, she says, "Yeah, we've begun meeting Monday nights at the café down the street, but it's Emily's birthday, so we're doing it today. Right now, actually."

Then I see what she scribbled: *Don't worry, that day is wrong. But tell him Monday. Whatever spy he sends will have nobody to spy on.*

I smile. "Perfect." Now I have something to tell Herr Becker. And, it'll give me a reason to go back to the House of Ministries *today*. I have an escape to plan. I take the letter from Monika's bed. "I'll let you go, then. Talk more soon?"

"Definitely."

She gives me a hug. I love her hugs. I love Monika. One last thought comes to me, something else I want to tell her. There's no way I'd ever leave her on this side of the Wall. She needs to know this. She needs to be ready.

Silently, I hook her pinkie with mine. Then I snatch her pen and write: *I'm planning an escape for us. Tell no one.*

CHAPTER 19

I'm smiling. Monika's reaction was the best. She slapped a hand over her mouth. I guess she didn't trust herself not to let a bunch of questions come flying out about how on earth I plan for us to escape.

Little does she know . . . I don't know yet.

I do know, however, that I'm going to call Herr Becker right away about Monika's Monday-night meetings. If he *was* listening, me calling him will prove that I'm a good little spy. I'm just not going to call right *right* away. All he'd know so far is that Monika and her friends meet *at the café*. He doesn't know which one. That means I have to give Monika enough time to have her meeting today before I reveal the café's location.

I also know something else. I'm going to lie through my teeth about what time I'm going to his office to have our own little meeting. I'l! give myself an extra hour, and I'll use that time to snoop around the House of Ministries.

I smile a little more at sticking it to Herr Becker in this way.

I practically tap-dance back to my apartment and into the bathroom. Tearing Monika's and my note as tiny as possible, I flush. Wait. Flush. Wait. Flush, until all evidence is gone.

After, I have time to kill before I make the phone call. My eyes fall on my Inventor's Box, and how the lid is still ajar from the too-big handlebar. I begin taking things out so I can reorganize. The broken swing, an arrowhead, the paint can, the leather purse and strap . . .

There's still more. A hammer. Rope.

Katarina and I have collected a lot over the years.

My tongue pokes out of my mouth as I arrange, but I finally get my treasures back inside the box with the lid closed.

Feeling accomplished, I'm ready to accomplish even more. I take a steadying breath. It's time to call Herr Becker.

It doesn't dawn on me until I've already got the phone to my ear that Herr Becker may not be working.

But a secretary is quick to answer. She's quick to tell me Herr Becker *is* in his office. He's there. At the House of Ministries.

I begin to enact my plan, saying I have something to tell him.

I picture Herr Becker salivating as his secretary relays the message. We agree on me coming in an hour, just as I had hoped.

I all but sprint out of my apartment. In my lobby, I nearly trip over the spool of cable the maintenance man has left in the middle of the lobby. At least the lift's chain is no longer stretched from wall to wall. The paternoster is moving again, too, even though the *Out of Order* sign is still hung across the opening to get on.

When I pass Katarina's building, my steps slow, debating about quickly filling her in, but I decide I don't have a minute to spare. I ramp up my pace, practically jogging. The weather is warmer today, with less of a bite in the air.

Outside the House of Ministries, I walk again, letting my breathing slow. The last thing I need is to stumble into the building gasping for air, baby hairs sticking up, and sweat dripping down my back.

I smooth my hair and take a step toward the building, then stop.

Can I do this?

Can I go creeping around the House of Ministries without getting caught?

All I really know is that I have to try. I wait for a man to enter and stay on his heels. Across the lobby, I follow him, using him to shield me as much as possible. I'm assuming Nasal Woman or someone will be looking for me at the time we established. But I came early. No one will be looking for me an hour early. The lobby is less busy than usual. I spot a man behind a front desk, his head down as he works. Another man heads in the direction of the public restrooms. When the man I'm following is greeted, I slink behind him and make a quick turn down a hallway.

I'm in!

I've thought about it, and if we want to make an escape from the building, we need to be as high as possible. We need to be on the roof.

In the stairwell, I go up, up, up until I see a sign for the roof.

Bingo.

So far, adrenaline has kept my nerves under control. But I pause again, afraid the knob won't turn, and I have to swallow. I look over my shoulder, expecting to see Herr Becker himself in the stairwell.

I'm alone.

I try the doorknob. It turns. With my lips in an *O* shape, I blow out a breath and step onto the roof.

Wind swirls my hair. There's a large stone next to the door. Mama once said how they used a rock to keep the door open at her work because the door automatically locked. She needed a key to get back in. I wonder if this door is the same? I grab it, just as it's nearly closed, and stick the stone in carefully to leave the door ajar.

Satisfied, I turn and let my gaze fully take in where I am. The House of Ministries isn't the highest building, but I'm pretty high up. There's about twenty or thirty steps from where I am to the edge of the roof. This portion of the roof sticks out almost like a nose. I need to get to the nostrils.

If anyone sees me from one of the neighboring buildings, my scheme will be ruined before I even get started. The best I can do is crouch. And hurry.

I bend in half and begin to run across the top of the black roof, directly down the center.

My heart pounds.

I feel exposed.

I hunch over more and run even faster.

At a roof vent, I pause, then take off again.

My footfalls thump against the roof.

I wipe hair from my face.

At the roof's edge, I drop to my knees and press my chest against my legs. I don't look up. I'm certain that when I do, someone will see me. I wait for a siren from a watchtower. I wait for dogs to bark. I wait for gunfire.

Nothing happens. No one sounds an alert that a girl is perched on the roof of the House of Ministries.

Slowly, I lift only my head. To my right, there's another roof vent, partially shielding me.

And straight ahead, there it is again: the West. There's the Coca-Cola sign. There's a slew of cars. We don't have many cars. Mama hasn't even bothered to apply to request one. But my goodness, there's so many cars. And they can go anywhere they want.

My eyes prick with tears.

Being over there would mean Mama is safe. Monika

is safe. Katarina and I can become whoever we want to be. I can be with my family.

Being over there changes everything.

And I'm going to figure out how. Right now.

I gulp in the biggest breath of oxygen possible while being bent against my knees.

I'm still shocked how close the West looks. Unbelievably close. But how far is it truly? That'll be important to know. I shuffle on my knees even closer to the edge of the roof to look over and down.

I immediately jump back. It's a long way to the ground, but there's a dog right below me. It's sniffing along the dirt. I inch forward again. There's a second dog sleeping in the shade.

Don't look up, I urge the sniffing dog. He slowly lopes toward the other dog and lies down. They're both black dogs and nearly blend in with the shadows.

One day in class, we determined the length of shadows, which is dependent upon the angle of the sun. There was an equation.

An equation . . .

Object height / tan θ = shadow length

Tan θ is the sun's altitude angle in degrees.

My teacher gave me and my classmates that number.

We calculated in the springtime, like it is now. And like it is now, it was after lunch. It may not be exactly accurate, but using that same number is the best I can do.

If only I can remember the number we used for tan θ.

I tap the side of my head, willing myself to remember. I breathe in more oxygen. And I remember it, happily banging my fist against the roof.

I also know this building is seven stories high.

In class when we were determining various shadow lengths, my teacher had given us an average height for stories, too. I wonder if Ava and my other family members have a mind for remembering numbers like I do.

Soon, I'll find out.

I calculate the length of the shadow beneath me where the dogs sleep.

It doesn't stretch all the way across the death strip.

From here, I'll have to guess. I'm not a fan of guessing. But if I repeat the shadow again and again and again . . .

I double-check.

I triple-check.

And I have a length from where I am to where I want to be in the West.

I know how far we need to cross. Thirty meters. Give or take.

Thankfully the death strip is narrower here than it is at other points of the Wall. And even more fortunately, this portion of the House of Ministries juts out pretty far.

Thirty meters.

That feels doable.

That's a hair longer than the distance between two bases on a baseball diamond. Our gym teacher had us do our thirty-meter dash from home plate to first base.

Now if only I could be like the aeronaut Sophie Blanchard and fly a balloon that short distance. We could rise up and glide over in no time. But being in the air long enough to go up and then over makes me nervous. Each second in the air is another opportunity for a watchtower to spot us and for the guards to train their guns on us.

There's also no way I'd ever be able to get the money to buy materials to make a balloon large enough. The basket would need to fit all of Katarina's family, Monika's, and my own.

No, a balloon is out.

But gliding is a thought. Katarina's Katharina Paulus

was a parachute jumper. We read in the aeronauts book how early parachutes were made from linen stretched over wood frames. I bet I could make that. I bet I could make one for each of us.

And the swing! I could attach it so Mama could have a place to sit. The handlebar could come in handy, too, as something to hold on to.

I bite my lip. Because I don't think it'd actually work. It's windy up here. But I don't think we're high enough. My fear is if we glide from this height, we'll fall too quickly. We'd never make it over the wall. We'd land directly inside the death strip.

Just the thought makes me shudder. We'd be sitting ducks. Trapped. With those dogs. They look peaceful while they sleep. But no part of me wants to see them awake and angry.

What we need is something to keep us on a straighter trajectory.

Kind of like how that man used a tightrope strung between two buildings. He walked across the cable.

Cable . . .

My mind darts back to the spool of it in my lobby.

Then my gaze jumps to the building across from me, the one with the jumbo-sized Coca-Cola advertisement.

What if I was able to attach the cable from here to there?

What if we didn't go on top of the cable but underneath it?

What if we rode beneath it, like a zip line?

CHAPTER 20

My mind is soaring as I crouch-run back inside, then down the many stairs, and toward the lobby.

A zip line.

Yes.

Yes.

Before I left the roof, I committed as much of it to memory as I could: the location of the vents, my best guess at the length and width of the roof, and the calculation I have of the death strip's depth. I'll sketch it all later to show Katarina.

But right now I have to focus on making it seem like I haven't been scheming on the building's roof the past hour. I have to somehow get outside the House of Ministries and then reenter at the time I told Herr Becker I was coming.

I poke my head into the lobby, scanning for Nasal Woman. A large clock tells me I have only two minutes.

Now, to get outside.

Or, I think, my gaze landing on the two side-by-side restroom doors on the adjacent wall, *perhaps I could come out of the women's restroom.* That way I don't need to cross the entire lobby.

I hug the wall, keeping my head down, and walk as discreetly as I can toward the restroom. So far, so good. My heart rate settles. Boy, has my heart had plenty of exercise the past few days. Calmer, I run a hand through my wind-swept hair, then I go to turn the knob.

Except, it doesn't move.

It's locked.

I'm screaming so loudly in my head I'm surprised my eardrums don't burst. Even as I think it, I know it's not possible. But it also doesn't seem possible that this door is locked!

"Fräulein Ziegel?"

I've been caught.

Slowly, I turn to face her. "Yes, that's me."

It's not Nasal Woman. This one has a deeper voice. "I didn't see you come in," she states.

I press my lips together, willing a genius idea to slip

out once I open my mouth again. I land on: "It was an emergency." I gesture toward the restroom. "I came in quickly. But it's locked."

"Of course it is." She checks her watch and lets out a sigh. "I have a key. Step aside."

I do, and Impatient Woman unlocks the door. I slip inside as quickly as possible.

I don't actually have to use the restroom, but I go through the motions of going into one of the many stalls, standing there for as long as seems necessary, flushing, then washing my hands.

When I emerge, all the woman says is: "This way. Quickly."

I follow Impatient Woman through the hallways, this time noting the right, left, up, up, up, up, right, left we make to reach Herr Becker's office.

At the last *up*, my mind starts spinning again at continuing up, up, up to the tippy top of the building. How would I attach the cable to the building? Perhaps wrapped around one of the roof vents. There were two, I remember. The cable is strong enough; otherwise the compartments in the paternoster would crash to the ground. Yikes. But are the vents strong enough to hold a dangling human being? My guess is Monika's papa is the heaviest.

Ahead, a man is knocking on a door urgently. He sees us approaching and motions to the door. "A little help?"

Impatient Woman sighs. From a pocket in her skirt she removes her set of keys again. She unlocks the door, shaking her head the entire time at the man. He thanks her and slips into what I glimpse to be the men's restroom.

"Hurry," she snaps at me, as if it were my fault this man forgot his key.

At Herr Becker's office, I take a big, deep breath before entering.

"Sophie," Herr Becker begins. I can't help but notice how he uses my first name this time. I ended the last conversation we had as *Fräulein Ziegel* while he was threatening me. "I must say, I wasn't expecting to hear from you so soon."

I force myself not to fidget in the chair. "I'm sorry, I thought you wanted me to call right away if I learned anything."

He smiles. "That I did. Now what is it that you'd like to tell me?"

My thoughts are still on the roof . . . After the cable is around the vent, how will I get the cable over the death strip? It's not as if I can walk the cable across and throw it over the wall to Ava to attach on her side.

I realize Herr Becker is staring at me. "I visited Monika," I spit out. "I went over to talk to her, thinking she might say something important."

"And did she?"

Even though it isn't figured out yet, I still can't help picturing flying through the air, the death strip beneath me, going safely over the trip wires and snarling dogs to my grandfather's outstretched arms on the other side. It'd have to be at night. How we'll actually get to the roof after the building is locked at night is something else to solve. But once we're there, the darkness will help conceal us from the watchtower. One after another we'll go. "Um, yes," I say to Herr Becker, tearing myself away from the best daydream I've ever, ever had. "Monika mentioned when and where she meets with her new friends."

I tell him.

Herr Becker raises an eyebrow, and I consider this reaction. He loves to play games with me. I could've just passed a test—by telling him what he's already overheard from his bug. Or this information may actually be new to him. Maybe the bug died. Maybe the bug's reach doesn't extend to Monika's bedroom. In that case, I could've just passed a different test—where I'm a useful spy to the Stasi and where Mama and Monika won't find their way into the back of an unmarked delivery van. Not yet anyway.

"Is there anything else you'd like to tell me, Sophie?"

I'm still Sophie.

It confirms that he's pleased with me. My thoughts jump again to the escape. Mama can use the swing seat I found as she's zip-lining. The bike handlebar, too. If it's put overtop the cable, it should slide down the cable, with Mama beneath it holding on. The swing, dangling from the either side of the handlebar, will not only give Mama a place to sit, but also distribute her weight evenly. That'll keep the handlebar from tipping to one side or the other. Inwardly, I smile at how my plan has come to life secretly in my head. Out loud I say, "No, that's all I learned. Monika and I didn't talk very long."

Because she was off to meet her friends. But I don't tell him this. I feel emboldened to keep this from him.

I feel emboldened that moments ago I was secretly on top of his building.

Herr Becker only stares, his lips pressed together. I don't blink. His eyes seem darker today, like his pupils are larger than ever. I once read how the pupils dilate like this when an animal is hunting, and I have the urge to reposition in his visitor chair. Before I give in to the instinct to squirm, Herr Becker reaches for his phone. He relays the information to someone. The entire time, his eyes never leave me. Mine never leave his either, as much to be brave but also because a prey would be stupid not to keep a close eye on a predator.

Herr Becker replaces the phone. "Thank you, Sophie."

"I'm happy to help."

He cocks his head. I may be imagining it but his irises are nearly gone as he says, "Are you?"

It feels like I've been punched in the stomach. I've said the wrong thing. I got caught up in fooling him and I messed up. He knows I'm not *happy* to be here with him. Nervous, I lick my lips. "I mean," I begin slowly, "I'll do whatever I have to do to keep my mama safe."

He nods. "You're excused."

I stand, my legs feeling as if I haven't used them in hours, and begin to leave.

"Sophie."

I freeze.

"You've proven yourself. As a result, I'll expect more out of you. Much more."

CHAPTER 21

Once I'm out of view of the House of Ministries, I shake like a dog that's trying to get the rain off. It gets a few odd looks from people passing by. But they'd be doing the same thing if they had Herr Becker as a *friend*.

But not for much longer, I remind myself.

When I left my building earlier, the paternoster was nearly fixed. I quicken my pace, afraid the maintenance man, and more importantly his spool of cable, will be gone by the time I get back to my building.

But it's there!

Problem is, so is the maintenance man. I take my time opening our mailbox that's lined up with all the others in the lobby. Empty. The man's back is turned, watching as each paternoster compartment circles up, then down. The spool of cable is sitting there for the taking.

I do exactly that.

I've never stolen before. I've only ever found lost treasures. The weight of having this spool, about the size of an overfed cat, feels heavier and heavier each speedy step up the stairs. But I keep going; I have to. There's too much riding on this cable.

So much *will* be riding on this cable—literally.

I barrel into my apartment only to stop short. Mama is home from work. She's sitting on the floor with her legs crisscrossed, surrounded by what looks like an endless amount of plants.

Suddenly, I feel the rattling of the nearby underground train. Two of the pots clink together and Mama steadies them.

This is strange, even for her. We keep a petunia pot, along with a cornflower plant and bluestar flower by the living room window. But judging by what's in the large box and what Mama has already taken out, there are way more potted plants than window space.

"What is all this?" I ask. "How did you get all these up here?"

With the lift broken, Mama herself had to take the stairs. That is no small feat for her and probably why she's unpacking the box from a seated position instead of standing.

"Hello to you, too," Mama says, but not unkindly. She nods to the spool of cable I'm carrying. "Off treasure-hunting again?"

"Um," I begin, buying myself time to think. I feel weird standing, and I join Mama on the floor. The large box of plants is between us. "It's from downstairs."

"That much I know. I nearly wheeled into it when I came in. Herr Stein was nice enough to send up my plants and wheelchair on the paternoster. Glad it's finally almost fixed."

Now I feel even worse for stealing from the nice man, especially since Mama is figuring he *gave* me his extra cable.

She misjudges my flustered expression, saying, "I know, I may have overdone it with the plants." She laughs. "I was on my way home and got to thinking about how . . . Actually, Sophie, would you mind putting some water in a pot for dinner?"

Not really for dinner, I know, but to conceal our words from being overheard.

I jump to my feet and run to the kitchen, bang a pot into the sink, and flip on the faucet. I don't *think* Herr Becker has bugged our apartment, but Mama also likes eliminating the chance of any neighbors over-hearing us.

Mama smiles at my return. "I got to thinking about how your grandfather is coming for Easter. He *loves* plants. I can only imagine what he'd think if he walked in here and saw only a couple around. When I grew up, they were *everywhere*. There was even this time I hid stamps under the soil of one of my plants. I was helping Sophie—my friend Sophie, that is—buy stamps to mail a batch of her White Rose leaflets. But then your aunt Brigitte found them. I was sure she was going to rat me out to your grandfather. In the end, she ended up helping me." Mama runs her fingers through her hair. "Lots of memories, darling. And to think, your grandfather and aunt are coming here. I never imagined that this would be happening."

Mama doesn't ever talk this much. Her eyes are even wet. I say, "I'm so glad they're coming."

Mama smiles. "Me too, darling. It's all come as such a surprise—you seeing Ava not once but twice. And now our family is coming *here*." Mama takes another plant out of the box.

"Uh-huh," I say. Even to me my response sounds off, but Mama doesn't look up. I should tell her. I should tell her that when Ava comes here on Easter we're going to finalize the escape plan. I should tell her that we're going to zip-line down the spool of wire that I stole—if it's enough. I'm dying to unroll it to see how much cable there is.

But I can't tell Mama any of this. Not yet.

Mama is *so* happy right now unpacking her absurd number of plants, and as much as she wants me to have a life in the West, I know her and I know she'll tell me that we should feel fortunate that our family has been given approval to visit us. She'll say that they'll be back on Christmas, then next Easter, and on and on.

That may be enough for her, but it's not for me. I look over my shoulder at the spool of cable. I'm a scientist. An inventor. I know Mama wants that for me, too. I grab a plant from Mama's box and say, "Is it okay if I put this one in my room?"

"Sure," Mama says, still distracted. I reach for a bluestar flower, and Mama adds, "But don't forget to water it."

I won't. But if I have my way, these plants aren't going to have me to water them for long.

CHAPTER 22

In the morning, I rush outside to meet Katarina. I have *so* much to tell her. Last night, I measured the cable to see if it was enough. It was! I also sketched out a schematic of the roof and the cable stretching from the roof vent to the Coca-Cola building.

Then I remember she has an early dentist appointment. In class, I debate leaning across the aisle between our desks and whispering about the zip line and the cable, but there are too many ears nearby.

I can't imagine our school is bugged, but I also never imagined I'd be a spy or that I'd be *actually* planning an escape over the Wall in a way that wasn't completely silly. This isn't a rocket or catapult. This is a legitimate way we can get across. And I need to tell my best friend.

Though . . . even if I leaned closer or snapped a finger next to her ear, I'm not sure she'd hear me right now, because . . . Anton. He's got her full attention. I'm stuck with ants in my pants until the final bell of the day. I grab Katarina's hand and practically drag her outside.

"Relax, Soph, where's the fire?"

I say, "I've been dying to talk to you."

Katarina grows serious. "Did something happen?"

"You could say that."

"Spill it already, then. Let's walk and talk."

She leads, and I rub my forehead. "I'm not even sure where to start."

"The beginning?"

"Right. All right, well, Monika knows."

"Knows?"

I twist my head, making sure everyone else pouring out the school isn't close enough to hear. "That we're escaping."

Katarina's lips pucker like she's about to say *What?* But I raise a hand to stop her. "There's more. Monika and I had a fake conversation so I'd have stuff to tell Herr Becker. Then I went to the House of Ministries. Then up to the roof. Decided we'll zip-line across." I hold up my hand again, anticipating Katarina's response. "I stole some cable from my lobby that we'll zip-line on. Then we have the handlebar and the swing seat. We'll need more treasures for the rest of us to use. Oh! And I almost forgot. My family is coming for Easter to visit. They got visas. So we have to have *everything* figured out by then so that we can tell Ava the plan."

Katarina stops walking. Her chin is jutted out. "Um, is that all?"

I take another few steps before I stop. Then I laugh. I laugh like she's told the funniest joke I've ever heard. I may be losing my mind. Or rather, there's been too much on my mind. "I told you it was a lot."

"Where do I even start to respond to all *that*?"

I smirk. "The beginning."

We begin walking again.

"Funny. Okay, so . . . Monika. How did she respond to the fact we're"—she lowers her voice, even though no one is near us anymore—"escaping?"

"She couldn't really respond because we weren't sure if Herr Becker could hear us."

Katarina presses on her temples. "My head might explode."

"Welcome to my world."

"Soph, your world *is* my world. So what was next? You were on the roof? How? When?"

"Yesterday. I snuck up, and we'll have to find another

way to sneak us all up there on the day we escape. There's no lift either."

We both know what this means: Mama will have to walk up seven flights of stairs.

She blows out a breath. "We'll help her. Don't worry, Soph. But then once we get up there, we're going to zip-line?"

"Uh-huh."

"Guess that's safer than the catapult."

I smile. "I've got the cable. Now we have to figure out how we'll get the cable from our roof over the wall so that Ava can secure it to something over there. There's a building right on the other side. It has a window. Maybe Ava can somehow attach the cable to it and we can zoom right through the window to safety." I motion with my hand.

"Zoom through a window, Sophie?" Katarina shakes her head in disbelief.

I laugh. "Hey, where are we going right now anyway?"

Katarina blushes.

"Katy?" I press.

"Well, I actually spoke to Anton today."

I slap her arm playfully. "You did what? Why didn't you tell me?"

"It literally happened right before the bell. Then as soon as I saw you, you practically jumped me."

"What did he say? Did you talk to him? Or did he talk to you?" By my last question, my voice is two octaves higher than usual.

"He talked to me! He just wanted to make sure I was okay from when I went flying into his lap. But then . . . he invited me to come watch his archery practice today."

My mouth hangs open. "Only a week ago, this would've been the biggest news ever."

She laughs. "Right?"

"So that's where we're going?"

She bobs her head excitedly.

The archery field is only a few blocks from our school, set up on an overgrown baseball field. As we approach, I see the archers in a line, each holding a bow and with a bag of arrows across their backs. The first boy steps up to where the home plate would normally be and shoots toward a target that's placed at first base. Too bad for him, he misses. He then pivots and shoots toward a target that's where second base would be, and then toward third base. He finally hits the third target, actually almost dead-on.

Katarina and I stop at a fence surrounding the field.

I prop my chin on my hands to watch. Anton steps forward next, and Katarina grips my arm like she can't stand the anticipation. He pulls back his bow, then releases the arrow. I watch it fly toward the target.

Anton hits the target, but I'm not sure where. My mind is registering something else . . .

I watched the arrow fly to the target.

I watched the arrow fly to the first base of a baseball diamond.

I watched the arrow fly *thirty meters*.

I grab Katarina's arm right back.

CHAPTER 23

"Ow, Sophie."

"Sorry."

After I release her arm, she rubs her skin. "What was that about?"

"The length between first base and second base is close to thirty meters. When I was up on the roof," I tell her, "I estimated by using the building's shadow that we'll have to get over about thirty meters."

She slowly shakes her head. "Thank goodness for Herr Wagner's class last year."

I nod. "Anyway, I wasn't sure *how* we'd get the cable that far."

She's the one nodding now. "Simply throwing it wouldn't work. You'd have hardly any trajectory because of the drag from all the cable itself. Thirty meters you said?"

"More. There's extra for us to attach it around our

side to a roof vent. I'm not sure how Ava will attach it yet on her side."

"I'm sure she can figure out that one little detail. You got yourself onto the roof of the House of Ministries, Sophie. You're kind of my hero."

I laugh. I needed it. Everything has felt so intense lately. Leave it to my best friend to make me feel like I can do this. I *can* get us over the Wall. I point to Anton, more specifically to one of his arrows. "If we attach the cable to an arrow? Maybe tape the cable to the entire length of the arrow? Then shoot it? I wonder if that'd do the trick."

"Guess we have to test it. That's the next step in the scientific method, after all."

"You're right."

She drums her fingers against the fence. "And you said your family was coming for Easter? That's less than two weeks away, and . . . well . . . no offense, but you aren't the most athletic of people. Do you even know how to shoot a bow and arrow?"

"Who says I have to be the one shooting?"

"I'm even *less* athletic. It has to be you. Unless you want me to ask my papa if he can do it?"

"No," I say. "I don't want anyone else to know about our plans. Not yet. Like you said, it needs to be foolproof first or else our parents won't take us seriously. We need to learn how to shoot. But you know what that means, right, Katy?"

I glance toward the archery practice.

Katarina follows my gaze, then focuses again on me. "What?"

"You need to talk to Anton so he can teach us."

Her face loses all its color.

"You'll do great," I reassure her. "He asked you to come watch him. He *wants* to talk to you."

"No, he *wants* me to stand here and watch him. That doesn't require me to use my voice, unless I decide to cheer for him. Which I won't. In fact, shouting at someone right as they are about to release an arrow probably isn't a good idea. So there. That's settled."

I've never had a crush before. I imagine I may some-day. But I can also easily imagine not ever having one. Katarina, though, has liked Anton since the first grade. As if he can hear us talking about him, he looks over. He waves. I say, "See! That was the invitation to come say hello after practice is over."

Katarina scratches along her hairline and says, "I don't know."

"I do. And you should probably wave back."

She does, but my best friend looks like she's being pinched as she does so. I'm glad I've never had a crush.

Until the end of practice, I pump her ego. By the end, she's rocking on her heels, as if she's trying to convince herself to jump off a cliff.

"Think of that episode of *Today at the Krügers*. Remember the one where the Monika character was scared to talk to her crush?"

"Maybe," Katarina says.

"You do. It's the one where she bit the bullet and talked to the boy and then found out that it got easier and easier each time she did it."

"Maybe," she says again.

I roll my eyes. "It's going to stay hard to talk to Anton until you just do it."

With that, I look over and the boys are beginning to leave practice. Anton looks our way—well, Katarina's way—and I seize the moment.

"We're doing this," I say. "I'll drag you if I have to, but it'll look really embarrassing."

"I hate you," she says between her teeth.

"Do not. Now, let's go."

Thankfully, she starts walking along the fence with me toward the opening behind home plate.

"You came!" Anton says to Katarina. "Hey, Sophie. It's cool you came, too."

"You're really good," I say to him. "Don't you think so, Katy?"

"Uh-huh."

Anton beams. "I've been doing it for years."

I decide to plant the seed. "We'd love to learn. It looks really fun."

"It is." Anton pushes some hair away from his eyes. What he doesn't do is offer to teach us.

I look around him to where his coach is dismantling the targets. "How far can you shoot?"

"And hit the target?" He laughs.

Katarina giggles.

At least it's *some* kind of a response.

"Sure," I say.

"I'm pretty accurate up to thirty or forty meters, I guess. I'm getting better. The target today was around thirty."

That I know.

"But if I'm just shooting to shoot, the arrow can go really far. Like three hundred meters."

"Wow," Katarina says.

Thatta girl.

Anton focuses all his attention on her. "You can try sometime, if you want."

I elbow her.

She doesn't respond.

I elbow her again.

Katarina stumbles forward a step. "I'd love that."

"Great," Anton says, smiling.

"Maybe tomorrow after your practice?" I chime in. "If it's okay, I'd really like to try shooting, too."

"Um." Anton looks over at me. "Yeah, I guess that's okay."

I say, "Perfect!" and link my arm with Katarina's. "Katy can't wait."

That earns her another big smile.

We make our exit. Neither of us say a word until we're off the field and back on the sidewalk.

"That went great," I say. "I'm sorry I did so much of the talking."

She shakes her head. "Please. I should thank you. I was tongue-tied."

I bump her with my hip. "You did great."

"Don't lie to me, Soph."

I laugh. "You'll do better tomorrow."

She finally cracks a smile.

We continue toward home. When we turn down one of the final blocks, it dawns on me the café is farther down this road. The café where the Stasi agent is supposed to be eavesdropping inside on Monika and her friends. I imagine him discreetly sitting there, sipping on some really bad coffee. I imagine him getting angrier and angrier with each wasted moment. I even imagine him calling Herr Becker and saying my tip was bogus.

Tomorrow may bring more than an archery lesson. It may also include a summoning from Herr Becker, demanding answers from me.

Or what if the summoning from Herr Becker doesn't wait until tomorrow?

Katarina and I say our goodbyes outside her building, and now as I get closer and closer to mine, I can't shake the fear that Herr Becker could be waiting for me inside my apartment.

He's done it before.

He could do it again.

And what if he's there and he starts poking around? Will he think the spool of cable is odd? Or my Inventor's Box?

Maybe he even already knows about my treasures,

if he snooped around last time he was in my apartment. He had time to make coffee, after all.

Frustrated, I let out a small scream as I pull open the door to my lobby, startling one of my neighbors who's leaving. "Sorry, Frau Wagner," I mutter. Her husband is one of my teachers.

She offers me a polite smile.

And I offer to hold the door for her, putting on my best *I'm totally fine* smile for her in return.

In the lobby, I blindly step onto the paternoster. It's not until the second floor comes and goes from my view that I realize it's working again. I step off at my floor and head toward my apartment. Outside, I eye the door suspiciously, looking for any signs that someone other than Mama and me has opened it recently.

But it's not as if I can tell anything.

I take a steadying breath, unlock the door, and turn the knob. The door opens a crack. It's dark inside. I listen for any sounds.

Nothing.

"Mama?" I call, but I know she shouldn't be home for at least another hour.

Not moving my feet, I give the door a shove. It flies open and bangs against the wall.

Nobody.

"You're losing it, Sophie," I mutter to myself.

But a little voice tells me that I have every right to be paranoid.

I take a step forward and something crinkles beneath my shoe.

Jumping back, I see I stepped on a piece of paper.

It's folded in half. It says *Sophie* on it.

Someone slipped it beneath our door.

CHAPTER 24

I quickly close the door to my apartment. With a shaky hand, I bend to retrieve the paper.

I've licked my lips so much over the past few days and weeks, they've grown chapped.

Please don't be from Herr Becker.

I repeat it in my head.

Over.

And over.

And over.

I open the folded paper, and relief floods me. Instantly, I recognize Monika's handwriting. I lean against the door, letting myself droop until my butt hits the floor. Then I begin to read. Monika is dying to know more about my escape plan. Has it really only been a day since we had our fake conversation? It feels like so much longer. It also feels like I could curl up in bed and sleep for a week.

Monika has so many questions. Who and how and when and where?

I don't have all the answers yet, though.

Monika says to slip a response under her door at exactly seven in the morning tomorrow.

Should I?

It's not that I don't trust Monika. But it feels dangerous to put down on paper what little I do have of a plan.

Speaking of which, I begin tearing up her note as I stand and head toward the bathroom. Time to get rid of what little evidence there is before Herr Becker can use it against us.

I'm up before my alarm.

I tossed and turned all night, debating whether or not I should put my plan on paper. But Monika has good ideas. She may be able to help.

The very first thing I write:

YOU CAN'T TELL ANYONE ANY OF THIS. PINKIE SWEAR!!!

We already pinkie-swore once. But it can't hurt to do it again.

Then I explain it all: the House of Ministries, the zip line, the cable and archery. I explain about my cousin.

I give the whole thing a name: Escape Night.

I smile, thinking how Monika's mouth will probably fall open. She'll have to be impressed with what we've done so far. Frankly, I can hardly believe it myself.

I realize while writing that we'll need a bow and arrow to use the night of our escape. There's still getting into the building that night, too. As far as when this is happening, that'll be figured out on Easter, when my family is visiting. I need to talk to Ava.

My blood is pumping with nerves and excitement by the time I'm done writing it all out.

I end it with:

DESTROY THIS.

Out of habit, I fold it the same special way I would any note that Katarina and I write during class. There's a pull tab on one side to open. On the other side, I write *Monika.*

I have thirty minutes to seven.

In no time, I'm ready for school. With my schoolbag on, Monika's note inside, I perch on the edge of my bed and stare at my alarm clock as it ticks closer and closer to our handoff time.

Sitting still is bad for me. It gives me time to doubt my plan. What if neither Katarina or I can learn to shoot a bow and arrow? What if we can't get to the roof? *How* are we even going to get into a locked building at night?

I dig in my desk drawer for lip balm and plaster my lips with it.

When I have three minutes to go, Mama calls for me. "Sophie!" she says from the kitchen. "Come give me a kiss. I'm about to leave for work."

I find Mama not at the door ready to leave, but in her wheelchair at the kitchen table. She's using transparent tape to cover a small crack in one of her planting pots. Even just seeing the many plants around sets me on edge. I now have one week and five days to finalize the plan before Ava gets here. And in the meantime, there's only four days until my next official meeting with Herr Becker. That is, unless he taps my shoulder before then.

I hate thinking that he can show up here whenever he likes and I won't know what I'm walking into. I don't want to come home again and not know if it's safe to walk into my own apartment. What if Monika responds with a note and he sees it? It'd give him more ammo in which to play mind games with me. Or . . .

arrest us all. If only there was a way to *know* if someone goes inside our apartment.

Mama tears off more tape and fixes it over another portion of the crack. I look at the clock. I need Mama to get out of here. We can't leave the apartment at the same time. She'll wonder why I'm stopping at Monika's door and what I'm slipping beneath it.

She finishes positioning the tape. "All done," she says. "Now to see how well this tape holds."

Tape . . .

Mama's use of it gives me an idea to solve my Herr Becker problem. But only if Mama leaves the apartment before me.

I kiss her cheek. "Have a good day, Mama."

She wheels—ever so slowly—away from the table. "See you tonight," she says as she crosses the room to the door. I mentally push her along. She pauses at the table by the door to grab her purse.

Gooooo.

There's only one minute now until seven.

As soon as Mama leaves, I tear off some tape the length of my thumb. My schoolbag's already on. I run toward the door but then gingerly open it, poking out

201

my head to see if Mama is down the hall. I watch as she rolls onto the paternoster.

Once she disappears, I race toward Monika's door. I'm tempted to drop to my hands and knees and see if I can spot her feet on the other side. But I trust that she's there and not someone else in her family. It's why she gave me a specific time. I begin to slide my note underneath and feel the tug from the other side, Monika pulling it through.

I do a double tap on the floor as a hello.

The tape's still on my finger.

I double back to my door to execute my plan to see if anyone but me opens this door.

I roll onto my tiptoes and align the tape so part of it is on the doorjamb and the other side of the tape is on the actual door. If someone opens the door, the tape won't hold. It'll tear away from the door.

I take a few steps back from the door, admiring my handiwork. The tape is transparent and blends right in. Now let's hope it looks *exactly* like this when I return home from learning how to shoot today.

CHAPTER 25

"We can do this," I say, tucking my hair behind my ears. I believe that . . . right?

Katarina makes a coughing plus laughing sort of sound. "If you say so."

She's got me. I'm not so sure. I say, "It's not like we have any other option but to learn how to shoot those things."

We're at the fence again, watching Anton and the other boys practice. The sun's so bright I have to squint. I'm getting sweaty, too, perhaps as much from the idea of shooting an arrow as from the warming temperatures.

"What if I shoot it backward?" Katarina poses.

"Is that even possible?"

She throws up her hands. "We can ask Anton, but then he'll look at me like I'm a moron."

I can't help but laugh. Katarina is *so* far from being a

moron. She's probably the smartest person in our entire grade. I grab her hand and pump it. "We can do this."

As if on cue, practice ends. The boys start to scatter, leaving only Anton behind with his bow and arrow. I'm not sure if he owns it or borrows it from the school.

The coach begins to pack up the targets, too. They're basically art easels holding round boards. The boards then have a black ring, with a smaller blue ring, an even tinier red ring, then a yellow circle at the very center. I know enough about archery to know the yellow circle is the bull's-eye.

Anton runs toward the coach, motioning to the last target.

The coach leaves it.

"Thank you, Anton," I say to myself. "Okay, let's go."

I call out a greeting. Katy silently waves.

"Hi, Katarina." His gaze lingers on her a moment before saying, "Hey, Sophie." He holds out the bow toward Katy. "Want to try first?"

She licks her lips. She's going to need some lip balm soon, too. We seem to both be sharing that nervous habit.

"I guess," she says, and takes the bow. She tests the

weight of it, raising and lowering it and switching from hand to hand. "It's heavier than I thought it'd be."

He laughs. "It's a youth bow. They get a lot heavier than this. But," he adds quickly, "you'll get used to it."

Katarina finally settles on holding the bow in her left hand.

"Oh, that's right," he says. "You write with your left hand, don't you?"

Anton just won himself some bonus points and I smile, but the moment passes when he adds, "I wish I thought of that before now. Shooting may be harder for you because of that. My bow is designed for right-handed people."

"Great," Katarina says sarcastically.

"But it really depends on which eye is dominant. If your right eye is dominant, then you'll want to use your right hand anyway."

I cup a hand over my brows to better see against the sun. "Is it possible for her to be left-handed but right-eye dominant?"

"Small chance," he says. "But let's see. There's something called a wink test."

Katarina's mouth drops open. I've seen her wink

before after she told me a really bad joke. It's not pretty. Judging by her face, she's thinking the same thing right now. No way does she want to wink in front of a boy she likes.

Anton holds up his hands with his palms facing out. He brings his fingers and thumbs together so that they overlap and a little triangle shape is formed in between his two hands.

"Start with your hands like this," he instructs Katarina.

She props the bow against her body to free her hands. We both copy him.

"Now look through the little triangle at the target." He glances over at me and Katarina, standing side by side.

"Close your right eye. Can you still see the target?"

The right side of my lip curls up as I try. "No," I say at the same time Katarina says, "Yes."

"Ugh, okay. Let's try the other eye anyway. Close your left eye. Can you see the target?"

From me: "Yes."

From Katy: "No."

"Katarina, looks like you are left-handed *and* left-eyed."

She sighs. "Can I still try it on my right side?"

"I mean, you can. But your center of gravity will be all off as you aim. You may as well be firing at a wall."

Which, I think, is kind of what we're doing. We don't necessarily need to hit the target, just get the arrow *over* the wall. It's more about distance, less about accuracy.

Still, Katarina's face is drooping. I hate seeing her feel like she somehow did something wrong when this is simply how she was born.

"Why doesn't Sophie go first?" she says.

"You sure?" I say.

"Please," she insists, and thrusts the bow at me. I take it, not wanting to upset her any further. "Now what?" I ask Anton.

Anton hesitantly steps closer, making our equilateral triangle into more of a scalene, with Katarina off to the right.

"First," he says, "put this on." He straps an arm guard on my left arm. "Now let's get you in a shooting position."

Anton turns his body so he's standing at a right angle to the target. His feet are shoulder-width apart, with his back foot slightly forward.

I copy him, leaving tiny footprints in the dirt until I'm in position.

"Do you feel comfortable and balanced?"

I glance at Katarina, then back at Anton. "Sure?"

"All right. Well, next we want to nock the arrow."

I clench my teeth together. Do what?

I quickly learn it means putting the back of the arrow on the string portion of a bow. The tip of the arrow will rest on this little shelf at the front of the bow. But first Anton puts this rubber thingy on the bowstring to apparently save my fingertips from pain. At this, I glance over at Katarina; she looks all too pleased not to be involved and hides a laugh behind her hand.

"Good," he says after some fumbling on my end to do the nocking. "Now we'll do something called a Mediterranean draw."

He might as well be speaking English to me.

But after his instructions, the first joint of my fingers are on the bowstring. My pointer finger is above the arrow, and then my middle finger and my ring finger are below. My thumb *should* be relaxed and down, not sticking up or out. My pinkie finger is supposed to do nothing. But it quivers, like it wants to do something to help in some way.

"Now, relax your bow hand. Remember, this isn't life or death."

I have to take a big inhale at that because, yes, Anton, it is. If I mess up firing the bow on Escape Night, our entire plan will go up in smoke. Literally, if the arrow sets off a trip wire.

Katarina steps closer, no doubt noticing how I'm shaking.

"Are you okay?" she whispers to me.

I nod, not trusting my voice.

She talks for me to Anton, "What does Sophie need to do next?"

"Get ready to shoot."

I raise my bow to the target.

I pull the bowstring back.

I aim.

I release the arrow.

CHAPTER 26

Well . . . I try to release the arrow.

"Let go," Anton urges. "Just let it go."

My arm begins to shake. "I'm scared."

He encourages me again, "Let go, Sophie."

"I can't."

"Anton?" Katarina asks.

"This happens."

"Soph," she says, "just open your fingers."

"Yeah!" Anton says. "Great suggestion, Katarina. Just act like you're dropping the arrow."

My arm is trembling from holding the bowstring back. I'm pushing away with my left arm. Am I even supposed to be doing that? I don't know why this is so scary to me, but it is.

I close my eyes, then straighten my fingers. I feel the arrow release.

"Good job!" I hear from Katy.

But when I open my eyes, it's clear Katarina is only trying to make me feel better. The arrow went practically nowhere. I could literally take five giant steps forward—diagonally forward, that is, since I didn't shoot straight—and I'd reach it.

Anton offers, "Most beginners are able to eventually get to eight to ten meters."

"That's it?" I practically scream the question at the poor boy.

"Farther after more practice. You're kind of close to eight. It helps if you pull the bowstring back *all* the way. You didn't have it anywhere near your face."

Because that's scary, too. What if the string scrapes off half my face when I release the arrow?

Anton laughs. "You look like I'm dangling a spider in front of you. You want the string touching your cheek. Or somewhere on your face or neck. It's called your anchor point. Once you find it, you'll want to pull the bowstring back to that same spot every single time. Oh, it also *really* helps if you keep your eyes open, too."

Were my eyes closed? I don't know. All I remember

is the weight of the bow and the fear of releasing the arrow.

Anton asks, "Do you want to go again?"

"No," I say, but I know I have to learn how to do this, so at the same time I nod yes.

Anton looks to Katarina for help deciphering me. "She wants to go again," she reassures him.

The one upside to my horrible start to shooting is that Katarina seems to be talking more and more to Anton. They're even standing next to each other now. Progress.

I need to make some progress, too, with getting this arrow to go at least thirty meters.

With a new arrow in hand, I set up again with Anton's coaching. "Pull it back," he says. "Pull it back to your face, Sophie. Seriously, touch the arrow to your face."

"Okay!" I shout. "I'm doing it."

Anton looks to Katarina again for support.

"You're not, Soph."

She walks forward to me and begins to pull back my arm.

"That's it!" Anton says. "But you need to open your eyes."

I blow out a breath.

"That's better. Don't close them again," he says. "I promise, it's not going to rip off your face or anything, if that's what you're thinking."

"It is," Katarina offers.

I turn to glare at her, even though she's not wrong.

The arrow turns with me, and Katarina screams.

"Forward!" Anton yells, and points. "Are you trying to kill us?"

"Sorry!" I follow it with another "Sorry!"

I face forward again.

I hear Anton take a big inhale. "Good. Never move your feet. It'll mess up your shooting stance." His voice lowers. "And put the rest of us at risk." Then louder: "Now keep your left arm straight and push. Push out the bow. That's it. Now hold it straight like that. Don't let your left arm bend. Steady. All right, now raise your right arm a little. No, no. Too high. Relax your shoulders. Lower. A little lower. Ugh, now you're off your face. Touch your face again. Good! Let it go! Release it!"

I can do this.

The arrow falls off the bow to the dirt before me.

No! After all that!

Anton covers his face and groans.

I groan, too.

"That was horrible," I say.

"It wasn't that bad," Katarina replies. Our arms are linked for our walk home.

"Says the girl who didn't try once."

Katarina snorts. "After how bad you did? Yeah, right. There was no way I was trying today, especially after you pointed that thing at me. Besides, did you see how well Anton and I were getting along?"

"I'm shocked he even invited us back. He must like you a lot."

"You think?"

I wink, and Katarina giggles.

But then I shudder at the thought of having to do this all again tomorrow. "Tomorrow will be better," Katarina assures me. "Promise. I'll even try shooting this time—and we *know* I'll be worse since I'm left-eyed or whatever."

"Let's hope not. Or else we may need to figure out a new way to get the cable across."

We both cringe and go the rest of the way to our apartments in silence.

In my hallway, I walk slower and slower. I stare at my shoes, hesitant to see what's coming. Will the tape be intact? Or torn away from the doorjamb, someone else inside the apartment? I always beat Mama home. Monika doesn't come anymore. I stop outside my door, quickly chastising myself for delaying. Finally, I look up.

The tape is intact.

The single win of the day. Herr Becker isn't here.

CHAPTER 27

Meet me after school in the park.

This morning, the rustle of a paper under the door right at seven alerted me to a note from Monika. School dragged, and I had to tell Katarina she'd have to start archery without me, but I've beaten Monika to the park and I now sit impatiently on a swing. She must want to talk about the escape. That's an easy guess.

But what specifically?

I can't imagine she'll want to talk me out of it. She's the one who first planted the idea of escaping in my head. She wants to be reunited with her grandparents as much as I want to be with my own family, maybe even more.

Maybe she has ideas to help. Maybe *she* even knows how to shoot a bow and arrow.

My knee starts bouncing from excitement, and I picture Mama going across the zip line on a seat just like this. All she'll have to do is hold on. If only we could all have a swing to use. I eye the other three swings on this particular set. I could take them. But I already feel bad about swiping the spool of cable from the poor maintenance guy.

But . . . my brain turns over an idea . . .

The paternoster he fixed uses the same compartment again and again. It goes up, around, down. What if I attach a long rope to the swing? Then, after Mama gets off the swing in the West—I pause, relishing how *in the West* sounds—I can pull the swing back up the zip line and the next person can use it. Even better, I already have a rope in my Inventor's Box.

"Whatever is going through your head right now, Soph, must be good."

I startle at Monika's voice. I didn't hear her walk up over the squealing little kids running around the playground.

She sits on the swing next to me.

"It's very good," I say. "I just got an idea that'll make Escape Night easier."

"Oh? Speaking of which . . ." Monika kicks off the ground, launching herself backward on the swing. "I one hundred percent want in. How is it that *I'm* the older of us, the one meeting with friends to talk about how much we hate it here, yet you're the one actually doing something about it? Remarkable, Sophie."

Remarkable? Me? "Don't go giving me a round of applause yet. There are still some massive pieces of the puzzle *we* need to figure out."

"Let's get to puzzling, then." She lowers her voice, despite the noise of the park. "You've got the escape location, the zip line, the cable, the idea to shoot the cable. Um . . . you mentioned the swing for your mama. What else is there?"

I also set myself in motion.

Monika goes forward as I go back. Both of our swings squeak, needing to be oiled. I give myself a few strong pumps, and for a few moments, we synchronize. It feels so good to have Monika back after days of not seeing her.

"The biggest problem is *how* we're going to get to the roof at night. The building will be locked after hours."

She points at me. "*That.* Can you get a key?"

"Seriously, Monika?"

She straightens her arms, leaning back on her swing. "When do you see your controller again?"

"I hate that word."

"Hate it or not, that's what he is."

"Three days," I answer.

"Keep your eyes open when you're there. Maybe he'll have his keys out on his desk."

"And then what? Ask him to borrow it for the night?" I give myself another hard pump with my feet, accelerating my swing. I forget about the key for now. "Getting inside is the first problem. A big one obviously. Plus, I'm awful at shooting a bow and arrow. I can probably jump farther than I can shoot. Katarina didn't even try yesterday, but I can't imagine she'll be any better. Can you shoot?"

Her eyes go wide. "I've never even held a bow. But I mean, I can try to learn. You said Anton is teaching you two. How is *that* going for Katy?"

"You'd be proud."

Monika smiles. She then begins dragging her feet, slowing herself. "Let me think on all this. I'm supposed to be at the pharmacy right now."

"Monika!" I chastise. "What if you get in trouble?"

"By the man over there?" she says, talking out of the side of her mouth. I follow her gaze. Beyond the kids going down the slide and the handful in the sandbox, there's a man with a newspaper on a bench. "He's been watching us."

For once, I'm not scared, I'm angry. "Let him. I'm

actually surprised Herr Becker didn't bring me in when he found out your meeting on Monday was a fake."

She bobs her head. "You'll need something to tell him. How about you say that you asked me here today to try to get some dirt out of me? That'll keep me out of trouble for being late to the pharmacy, too. Tell him that I told you that we changed the date last minute on Monday. Will that be enough to hold him over?"

"I don't know. He wants to know who your friends are and why you're meeting."

She stands, wiping her palms down her pants.

And I know she doesn't know what to tell me right now. The fake meeting time wasn't anything incriminating. But if she does tell me something that Herr Becker doesn't like, she'll find her way into the back of a delivery van again. This time, she might not return. The problem is, if I don't start giving him names, it's Mama who'll be in that truck.

"Go," I say, gripping the swing so hard my knuckles may break.

"I'll think of something juicy you can tell him. Promise." Monika hugs me. "Seven will be our time to give each other messages, okay?"

I nod. It makes me nervous, though. Each message is another opportunity to get caught.

As Monika leaves, she ignores the man reading the newspaper. I glare at him, but he's not watching me. His eyes follow Monika.

I won't let them have her.

I won't let them have my mama.

Remarkably, I'll get us out of here.

First things first, I need to get better at shooting. The baseball field is nearby. I quickly head in that direction. Hopefully, it's going well for Katarina, in one way or another.

I round a tree, and the baseball field comes into view, along with Katarina and Anton. She's at home plate, her body turned toward the target, but I can only see her back since she's shooting left-handed. That can't be going well, not with a bow made for a righty.

But she's trying.

Katarina pulls back the bowstring, and I find myself holding my breath, waiting for her to release the arrow.

This was the hardest part for me.

But within a heartbeat, she releases the arrow.

And, my mouth drops open.

The arrow soars straight off the bow with a *whoosh* I can hear from here.

Katarina is *good*.

She can shoot a bow and arrow!

Her arrow didn't make it to the target. But it got close. Closer than I was able to do. But with some practice . . .

I make a whooping noise and begin running toward my best friend.

Katarina spins her body to see me. Thankfully, she hasn't nocked her next arrow.

"I saw that!" I call.

She makes a squealing noise.

I give her a hug, with the bow between us. "How?!"

"Anton brought me a lefty bow."

"Anton Volker!"

I'm apparently unable to speak in full sentences or even at a normal decibel.

Anton grins. "She's a natural."

"A natural!" I parrot.

"Who knew?" Katarina says with her own grin.

Not either of us, that's for sure.

I could burst from excitement. And relief. For the first time, I have a renewed surge of hope that we can actually do this. We might actually escape.

CHAPTER 28

The House of Ministries looks even more like a fortress than it did the first time I came here.

One we'll somehow have to get inside on Escape Night.

I watch as people enter and leave. Many are likely going home for lunch. There's the main doors. There are also ground-level windows.

Could we break a window and climb through?

As soon as the option filters through my head, I reject it.

The Stasi wouldn't miss a broken window. There's a lot of important information in there. Files and things.

Like the files on me, on Mama, and on Monika.

If only I could get my hands on those files to destroy them.

Herr Becker left his office once before when I was there, but only for a second.

What if I could get him to leave for longer?

But for now, I better go inside. I feel the eyes of a border guard on me.

The lobby is surprisingly empty. There's a grouping of chairs to my left. Two are filled with people leaning close to talk to each other. There's the main desk, with a man behind it. Standing beside the desk is Nasal Woman. She's picking at her nails. Her foot taps impatiently. As if she can sense me, she looks up.

Nasal Woman offers no greeting today, only motions for me to hurry along.

We follow the same route as always. She turns sharply around a corner, revealing the keys swinging under her sweater. I'd forgotten she wears this zipcord-like contraption around her waist. Now that the keys are free, they jingle enticingly.

I have the urge to reach out, rip them off, and run.

I don't need to hypothesize if I'd be caught or not.

But there they are.

Too soon, we're at Herr Becker's office. Once inside, he doesn't waste a breath. "Monika and her friends weren't at the café like you suggested they would be."

I'm shaken by the fact he doesn't even say a hello. It's not like I expect him to comment on the weather. But it feels like he's a lion that's been waiting to pounce.

Still, I'm ready with a rehearsed line: "They changed the date. I didn't know until afterward."

"That's right. You and Fräulein Voigt had a play date at the park a few days ago."

I nod. Mid-squirm, I realize I'm squirming. I shove my hands under my legs against my chair and remind myself I prepared for this meeting. "I invited her there. I know you are expecting information from me."

He smiles catlike. "You'd be right."

Monika kept her promise and slid something juicy under my door.

Tell him one of my friends mentioned how she overheard a coworker talking about wanting to escape.

In reality, there is no coworker. It made sense to divert attention away from Monika to someone fictional.

I recite the lie to Herr Becker.

He steeples his fingers. I wish I knew what was going through his head. Abruptly, he yanks open a drawer and removes a key. Herr Becker crosses the room to his file cabinets and unlocks a drawer on the far-right side.

Herr Becker plucks a file from the drawer, then returns to his side of his desk.

He flips the file open and begins thumbing through pages.

Thanks to my new skill of reading upside down, I quickly read Monika's name.

I glance again at the filing cabinets. If *Voigt* is in that filing cabinet, I wonder if *Ziegel* is as well.

When I look back, I see the phrase *hostile person* and also *hostile-negative person* with a question mark.

I have no clue what these mean.

Monika isn't hostile. There isn't a mean bone in her body. Maybe the word means something different to them, though.

I also see a section that lists her family members. Next to her grandparents' names there is an annotation that they are in the West.

"Sophie."

My gaze jumps back to Herr Becker, who clearly saw me trying to read Monika's file. Heat begins in my chest and fills my cheeks.

"As you've taken an interest in my work, I believe it's worth repeating my two main objectives. The first is to stir out any conspiracies *before* they are even planned. The second is to stop any injustices against our party *before* they happen. If Monika and her friends are planning an escape, we must stop it before any harm can come to the party or them."

I shake my head so violently I feel a pain in my neck. "Not Monika. It was her friend who mentioned a coworker."

"Are all of them in this new circle of friends together?"

"I don't know."

"Hmm," he says. He flips through more pages in Monika's file and unearths a photograph of Monika with another girl.

"Is this the friend Monika was referring to?"

"I don't know," I say quickly.

"Sophie, take your time. I am willing to spend as long as needed with you this afternoon."

That's the last thing I want.

I also don't want to point fingers at Monika's actual friend, especially since the information I'm passing along isn't real. I say, "I got the impression it wasn't from a girl, but from a boy. A man. He was older, I think."

I'm lying through my teeth, and I hope Herr Becker doesn't realize it. Even if he did, would he let on?

I add, "I can try to find out."

"A name," Herr Becker demands.

I nod.

At that, Herr Becker closes the file.

I take it as a sign I'll soon be dismissed and shift

forward in my seat. My shirt is damp from sweat and peels away from the back of my seat.

But I've survived another meeting with Herr Becker.

I haven't implicated Monika or the girl in the photo.

I now know where Herr Becker keeps Monika's file.

And most importantly, Nasal Voice has the keys I need for Escape Night. Now to figure out how to get them from her.

CHAPTER 29

Sunday comes and goes.

This means there is less than a week to Easter.

This means that I have a single meeting with Herr Becker before my family comes.

And if I don't have a plan fully in place by then, then that's it. No Escape Night. Sunday will be *the* opportunity to talk with Ava and irreversibly set the plan in motion.

I may throw up.

"Sophie? Are you sure you don't want to try?" Katarina says, nodding toward the righty bow and arrow.

"It's you, Katy. You're our archer."

Anton scrunches his brows, probably very confused by my serious tone. For all he knows, this is just two girls wanting to learn a new hobby. Our school only has a team for boys.

Thankfully, Katarina has improved. A lot. Already,

she's able to shoot farther than most beginners. But she needs more practice. I'm not sure if the five more afternoons will be enough.

Anton lays a hand on Katarina's shoulder as she's lining up her next shot. I see him gently pushing and saying, "Relax. So much of archery is confidence and staying relaxed. You're good, Katy."

She smiles at that and exhales a long, slow breath.

Katarina releases the arrow and—yes!—it hits the target! It's not a direct hit, not even close, but who cares? Not me! All I care is that she's able to shoot the bow and arrow the distance we need. She just needs to practice until she can do that every time.

She lines up another shot and hits the target again.

I find myself releasing a slow, controlled breath as well.

This is going to work. Inside, I do a happy dance, a full-on jig, with my arms and legs flailing. I've never been a good dancer.

"You're doing great, Katy!" Anton cheers. "But remember so much can affect your shot. The weather, like the wind. The slightest wave of your bow makes a huge difference in the trajectory of the arrow. Or even the arrow's weight, if you're using a different arrow than what you're using now."

"A different arrow?" I ask.

"Totally," Anton answers. "The ones we have at school aren't the best. The ones the professionals use are a bit heavier. Just that little extra weight will change the trajectory Katarina is perfecting."

I see her swoon at his use of her name.

But my inner jig has abruptly stopped. Any extra weight can throw off Katarina's trajectory. Like . . . attaching a cable to the arrow.

How did I not think of that?

On Escape Night, she'll have a *single* shot. We can't risk the arrow falling short and setting off a trip wire. Or alerting the dogs. There's no second chance to adjust to a different weight or to the weather.

I slap a hand over my forehead and start rubbing.

"Soph?" Katarina asks. "Are you okay?"

"Sudden headache," I say. "Long day."

My best friend watches me a moment, but I point to the target. "Keep practicing?"

Her head bobs.

She pulls back her arm with determination and hits the target again.

Good.

But now my brain is stuck on how the cable is going

to affect the arrow. We need to practice with the extra weight. I already picture taping the cable to the entire length of the arrow to make the cable's weight even. But there will be drag. We need to test it. Katarina needs to practice shooting it this way. I growl inside my head; Anton will have some major questions if I bring the cable tomorrow afternoon.

I wish we could act openly in front of him, speak openly. But we can't. You never know who you can trust. If Herr Becker turned me into an informant, who's to say Anton isn't one, too? Or someone in his family. Anyone could be a spy. Didn't Herr Becker say he had many, many grown-ups who secretly work for him?

Katarina shakes her arm like a wet noodle. "I need a break."

Anton snorts. "You're officially an archer now, sore muscles and all. You know, bows and arrows have been used here in Germany for thousands of years. As early as fifty thousand years ago, archaeologists think."

"Wow," Katarina says.

Huh? I think, my reaction a bit different. We didn't learn about this in school. At least I don't remember.

"Anton," I say, "is anyone else in your family into archery?"

"My dad got me into it and suggested I go out for the team."

I say, "Oh? What's he do?"

"Like for a job?" he asks. "He works in a factory."

"Does he like it there?"

Katarina's eyes shoot daggers into me. She's probably wondering why I'm putting Anton on the spot like this, especially about someone's happiness within our party.

Anton doesn't show any anger, though. He only shrugs. "Never asked him."

"I see," I say. "I was only curious. Maybe I'm just nervous to see where I'll be assigned one day."

Actually, I asked because I'm curious about Anton's loyalties. It's interesting he knows something we haven't learned in school. Sort of like how Katarina and I know about the women aeronauts.

He nods. "I get that." He then asks Katarina, "How are you feeling? Do you want to practice more, or are you done for the day?"

I like Anton. I can see why Katarina does. I mean, I don't like him in *that* way. But he's nice. Helpful. It makes me wonder if he'll help us even more. "Katy, you look pretty tired, so maybe we should call it a day.

But didn't your papa say he wanted to see you shoot? Anton, do you think Katarina could borrow the bow and arrow for a few nights? She promises to take good care of it."

Anton hesitates.

"I promise," she says.

And this is why I love my best friend. She has no clue what I'm scheming—she's probably even a bit mad at me for asking Anton those questions—but she's still willing to go along with me.

Anton scratches the side of his head. "Umm, sure, I guess. We don't have any lefties, so it's not like anyone will need it at practice tomorrow. Just please don't lose it. Or let Sophie use it. Coach will have my head."

"Promise," Katarina says again. He lets her take the case with a nervous look. As soon as we're far enough away from Anton's earshot, Katarina whispers, "What *was* that?"

"We weren't thinking like true scientists," I say. "The cable is going to affect the arrow's trajectory. You're getting good. But we need you to be good at shooting it *that* way, too. And we can't practice that in front of Anton, can we?"

"How did we not think of that?" Katarina squeezes

her eyes closed. "I don't know if I can do it with the extra weight. I'm not even making it far enough every time." She adds quietly, "This is too much pressure. It's literally up to *me* to get the cable across or Escape Night is done. That's it. Stuck here forever. Or worse: stuck here forever in jail. All this for nothing."

My heart pinches. I wish I could reassure her, but the truth is that she's right.

"You've got to do it, Katy. What other choice do we have?"

CHAPTER 30

When Katarina's expression only gets darker, I add, "Hey, if I can't figure out a way to get the keys, the whole plan is off anyway."

I say it to try to take some of the pressure off her, but it only makes her shake her head in disbelief.

"This is too big for us. We need help. I think it's time we tell our parents. We're supposed to escape soon, Sophie. Like really, really soon. They'll need time to prepare, right?"

I scratch the back of my head. I've been nonstop itchy lately. "I just don't think we should tell them until we *know* we can even shoot that far."

"You mean if *I* can shoot that far."

"Yeah," I say meekly.

"Why not our parents, though? Maybe my papa can. Or your mama. If not our parents, what about Anton? I bet he could do it easily."

This stops me. "We can't tell Anton, Katy."

"Why not? You told Monika."

"That's different."

"What if she tells one of her new friends?"

I insist, "She won't. She wouldn't put us at risk like that."

"Whatever. But what if Anton wants to escape, too? He likes me. I've wondered if he does for what feels like my whole life and now I know he likes me back. Now you want me to just leave him forever?"

I scratch again, harder. "We can't tell him, Katarina. I'm sorry. What if he turns us in?"

"He wouldn't do that to me!"

"You don't know that for sure, do you? You've spent all of four afternoons with him. I'm a spy. Why couldn't he be a spy?"

Even as I say it, I don't think it's true that he'd turn us in. The fact he knew all that stuff about the history of bows and arrows makes me wonder if he's not happy with the life here either. But I can't tell Katarina that. We already have Katy, her parents, her brother, then Monika and her parents and brother. And my mama and finally me. That's ten people we need to secretly get over the Wall.

I knew the number was large. I've known all along

who we'd include in our escape. But I never counted it out this way.

Ten people.

Ten of us I'll have to get to the roof.

Ten times that one of us will ride the zip line.

Ten times someone could catch us in the act.

Ten times our lives will be at stake.

"There's ten of us!" I say to Katarina. "We can't have anyone else join us."

"So only *you* get to decide these things, Sophie?"

"What?"

"You decide when and where and who and how?"

I stomp my foot. "Katarina, stop."

She looks at my foot like I'm going to keep going, straight into a full-on tantrum. "Stop? Right, because *you* told me to?"

I feel a dizziness sweeping over me. "That's not fair."

"Nothing in this life is fair! I just got to know Anton and—because you say so—that's it!"

I avoid an eye roll. "You don't even know him. You act like you're married, but you talked to him for the first time last week!"

Katarina's hand finds her hip. She stares me down.

"We've spent every afternoon together since then. He writes me notes all day long. He called me last night."

This stops me. "He called you? Katarina, you better not have said anything that could get us in trouble. You know they listen to phone calls!"

Katarina throws up her hand. "Great! Now I have straw for brains, too."

"I wasn't saying—"

But Katarina isn't listening to me. No, she's walking faster. Her footfalls are so heavy the carrying case of the bow and arrow swishes behind her like a pendulum.

She's three steps ahead of me, then four. The gap between us gets bigger and bigger, until my best friend is practically running to get away from me.

I fall facedown onto my bed.

It's not until my nose squishes into my pillow that I realize I didn't even notice whether the tape was still intact.

Being in a fight with Katarina is messing me up. On top of everything else.

We've gotten into fights before. But always stupid,

little tiffs like the time I took the last slice of krusta without asking her if she wanted it. Is that what I'm doing now? Am I not thinking about what my best friend wants, but in a much, much more serious situation?

Ugh. I am.

I groan, but it's interrupted by another sound. Someone fiddling with the lock on the door.

Someone is trying to get *in*.

Every muscle in my body tenses.

It can't be Monika. No way she'd miss more training.

Mama should be working for at least another hour.

I think that maybe it's Katarina, wanting to work things out just like I do, but she doesn't have a key. She'd knock.

This person isn't knocking.

Did I do something wrong that's made Herr Becker want to check up on me? The fact I have to even ask myself the question makes me hate him even more.

I hear the lock turn.

I fall off the bed and crawl to my Inventor's Box. I quickly root through until I find the hammer.

The door opens.

With both hands, I grip the hammer and take

quick, sideways steps down the hallway and into the living room.

Mama.

It's only Mama.

My arm falls to my side, the hammer dangling from my hand.

"Sophie?" she questions. Her eyes on the hammer look alarmed. On her lap is a grocery bag.

I'm suddenly feeling foolish and say, "Sorry, I thought you were an intruder."

"An intruder?" She laughs, but in disbelief. Then her expression turns serious. "You look really shaken. What's happening here, Sophie?"

I want to tell her. I want to tell her so badly. I just need some more time.

Mama presses, "If you're worried or scared or *any-thing*, you have to tell me. It's my job to help you, protect you. Please."

I nod.

Mama eyes the hammer again. "I mean it."

"If I need help, I'll come to you. I promise."

Mama seems to accept my words. For now. "Well, I'm sorry for scaring you. The lab told me to leave early, so here I am. They said to take tomorrow off, too."

"What? Why?"

I remember what Herr Becker said to me the very first time we met.

It'd be a shame if your mother's job becomes too taxing or too tiring and she isn't able to keep up with the demands of her work.

Mama wheels farther into the living room, then into the kitchen. I follow her. She hoists the bag onto the table, stands to her feet, and begins to unpack it. "They said I've been working a lot and I could use a break."

"Really? It doesn't feel like you've been working more than usual."

"Not more hours. But I just finished a big project that required a lot of time and focus each day."

"And they said you seemed tired?"

Mama lets out a weird sound, like I've insulted her. "No, they didn't say anything like that. Just that I could use a break."

"But you said you completed your project? The work you're doing is good?"

Mama meets my eyes, her face a bit stern. "Of course it is, Sophie."

I nod quickly.

Mama takes a steadying breath, turning her focus

back to unpacking the food bag. "The timing is good anyway. With everyone coming for dinner in a few days, it'll give me time to get things in order."

Mama doesn't seem worried about the lab suggesting she take time off, but I can't help feeling worried. What if someone *told* Mama's boss to give her time off? What if Mama's so-called break is a warning from Herr Becker? And if so, why is he threatening me this time?

CHAPTER 31

Herr Becker is the worst, and the only person I want to tell this to is mad at me.

Not that I blame Katarina.

In my bedroom, I wring my hands.

I need to fix this with her. Katarina has always been there for me, and I need to be there for her in return. That starts with an apology—a big fat one.

Just talk to her. She's your best friend. She'll forgive you.

Slowly, I make my way to the telephone. Mama won't be happy if I go running off when I have homework to do, then dinner to help with. When I hear Katarina's voice on the other end, I say, "I'm sorry. So, so sorry. Very sorry. I was wrong and mean and horrible and will you please forgive me?"

Silence.

"Katy? Please. I really am sorry. I wasn't thinking about your feelings."

A small voice says, "You really weren't."

"Please forgive me. We're a team."

A second silence.

An even smaller voice. "I don't think I can do it."

"Shh!" I say quickly, not only to stop her doubts but to stop her from saying anything more on this phone line.

"I know," she says, an edge of anger to her voice again.

"Sorry! I know you can do it. Meet me outside after dinner? Let's finish our homework together. You're so much better at math than me."

Katarina exhales. Then: "Fine."

I close my eyes in relief, then return the handset to the cradle.

I feel a little better.

Katarina may not forgive me totally yet, but she's willing to see me. That's a start.

Outside with Katarina, I think about the scientific method and what we've done so far. Katarina and I have asked a question: *How can we get over the Wall?* We researched. We constructed a hypothesis: *We'll shoot across an arrow with the cable attached.*

Now to test our theory.

"But where?" I ask Katarina.

"I don't know." There's that edge to her voice again. I'm still not out of the doghouse. "But I don't want to be standing on the street with this thing."

She means with the carrying case for the bow and arrow on her back. I'm glad she brought it. I wasn't sure if she would . . . if Katarina has had enough of me and our crazy Escape Night planning.

I have the spool of cable, too. It's at my feet. I could argue I look more suspicious, but no way I'm saying so. Besides, Katarina's right. We need to get out of here before someone sees us. Separately, we both look odd. Together, we definitely look like we're up to something.

We don't need a neighbor getting too curious. Mama always says neighbors are some of the biggest tattlers.

Or what if someone was listening on our telephone call, knows that we'd be outside after dinner, and is already watching us?

I'm so sick of having this fear, of not knowing when someone is trying to spy on *me*. "Let's go inside and figure it out?"

Katarina nods, and we hurry into her lobby. "I've been thinking," she says. "If I'm going to shoot from a roof, I want to practice there, too."

"What? You want to go to the House of—"

"Don't be daft, Sophie."

I flinch.

"Sorry," she amends. "You're not stupid. Not at all. But I meant my roof." She looks up at the ceiling. "One of our neighbors has a bird he keeps up there. I hear it screeching sometimes."

"Do you think your neighbor is going to go up there tonight?"

"I don't know," Katarina says.

"Well, does he go often?"

"Don't know. Do you have a better idea, though? If we don't start taking chances, we're never going to get out of here."

By *out of here* I know she means the East.

I lick my lips. Good friends listen to each other. *Give and take*, I remind myself. I may not love the idea of getting caught by Bird Man, but Katarina is right. We need to start to take chances. "Let's do it. Lead the way, Katy."

Her building is taller than mine. I'm out of breath by the time we make it to the roof. It's nearly dark now, but it'll be dark on Escape Night, too. "There's a lot of space. You'll be able to shoot without the arrow flying off the roof and piercing someone in the stomach."

For some absurd reason, we both laugh. We laugh harder than we should. At the same time, we shush each other, which only results in more laughter.

"All this . . ." Katarina begins.

"It's so much," I finish.

She swallows. "But we can do this."

"*You* can do this."

There's a full moon tonight, casting a glow across the entire sky and roof. Katarina begins to unpack the bow, and I begin to unroll the cable. She says, "I guess we'll find out. It's kind of creepy up here."

The bird screeches. It's in a cage in the corner behind us. I refuse to look in that direction. I've never liked birds. "Very creepy," I say.

I focus on my task. Once the spool is empty, I lay the arrow and the tip of the cable side by side. I creep close to the bird's cage in order to lay out all the remaining cable. The bird screeches again. I nearly trip over the cable.

It's in a cage. You are not, I remind myself.

But even as I say it, I know I'm in a cage as well. And that's exactly why we're up here. I jog to the front of the arrow. At its middle, and at the arrow's tail end, and right before the fletching feathers, I wrap heavy-duty tape.

"It's secure," I say.

"It's heavy," Katarina says, bobbing the arrow in her hands. "Really heavy."

The light from the moon illuminates the doubt in her eyes. I bet I have it in mine, too.

The dang bird screeches again. "Quiet," I grumble. The last thing we need is Katarina's neighbor checking to see why his precious bird is worked up.

Katarina nocks the arrow into the bow, positioning the cable where it extends off the arrow to the side. I run my gaze over the length of the arrow that's left. There's so much of it.

"I'll just shoot straight, I guess?"

"And slightly up. The roof will be a lot higher than the wall."

Katarina nods, and I know she's picturing the arc and trajectory of the arrow. "Here goes nothing."

She releases the arrow, and her words couldn't be more true.

Here goes nothing.

The arrow barely goes anywhere. It drops from the weight and the drag of the cable after only a couple meters.

I scratch my head aggressively. "Maybe it'll help if

I hold the cable behind you?" I suggest. "That way the arrow isn't picking up the weight of the cable off the ground?"

Katarina nods and retrieves the arrow.

A few steps behind her, I hold the cable, spreading out my hands. That still leaves *a lot* of it on the roof.

I hold my breath as she tries again.

We both growl.

The arrow went farther. But not far enough. Not even close to far enough. It would've landed in the death strip. It could've set off the dogs in a barking fit.

"What are we going to do?" Katarina asks.

I throw the cable. "I don't know."

After testing a hypothesis, a scientist will ask herself: Is this procedure working?

The answer couldn't be clearer.

No, it's not. This isn't working at all. What now?

CHAPTER 32

I toss and turn all night, nearly making myself into a bedsheet mummy.

In the morning, I unravel.

The scientific method tells us to troubleshoot. To check all steps and our setup, and then to draw conclusions. I've run it all through my head and I conclude . . . the cable is too heavy. Katarina won't be able to get it off the ground, let alone the distance we need.

I dress for school thinking . . . *maybe something lighter?*

I have a rope in my Inventor's Box. I could attach the rope to the arrow, then the end of the rope to the cable. After the rope is in the West, Ava can reel in the rope, bringing the cable to her side. She'd then just have to attach the cable for us to zip-line across.

It could work.

But when I hold the length of it in my hand, it feels . . . substantial. It's not so much lighter than the cable. But we'll try it. We have to explore all options, try everything, and ask all the questions.

I just already know the answer. And we're running out of time.

I stuff the rope back in my box and notice it's almost seven: the time Monika and I exchange notes. Maybe she can help. I quickly tear a piece of paper from my notebook.

I scribble:

Cable too heavy to shoot across. We need lighter. Much lighter. Any ideas?

I pause, my pencil above the paper, doubting if I should risk another note that could end up in the wrong hands. But Monika can help, I hope.

Outside the baseball diamond, I lean against a tree in the shade. My eyes begin to droop.

Thwack.

My eyes pop open.

Anton is jumping up and down. Katarina's smile is huge, easy to see, even from here. Did she hit a bull's-eye? I squint at the target. It's hard to tell, but if she didn't hit the thing dead-on, she got close.

I'm so happy for her. I'm proud of her.

Katarina is doing her part.

It's me who is stuck. I bang my head against the tree trunk, hoping it'll shake free an idea and also keep me awake. But it only hurts.

I'm supposed to be thinking. Troubleshooting. Problem-solving. Instead, all I'm doing is giving myself a bump. I sit up straighter and drink more of my water instead. H_2O increases the brain's temperature and gets rid of brain toxins and dead cells. I also read water can help to regulate stress and anxiety.

I chug from my bottle, not sure how long it takes for this liquid gold to kick in and do its magic.

What is light enough to shoot on an arrow?

How am I going to get everyone into a locked building and onto its roof?

Tired of the same old problems, I think about what will, hopefully, come after Escape Night instead.

It's been less than twenty days since I saw Ava outside the theater and only two weeks since our secret talk. But it feels like forever since I've seen her. Once I'm in the West, I'll be able to see her every day.

Katarina, Ava, and I will be the best of friends. Though Ava likely already has a best friend. We'll be a group of four, then.

The Fantastic Four.

Oh, oh. The Fun-tastic Four.

I wonder if Ava is also into science. It runs in the blood, after all.

I wonder if her favorite color is green, like me. Or maybe purple, like Katy.

I wonder what new television shows she'll introduce us to, what books, what games.

I wonder, I wonder, I wonder . . .

All that water chugging has made me need to use a bathroom.

Great.

The café where Ava and I met for our secret conversation isn't far. I jump up, happy the café doesn't lock its restroom like the House of Ministries does. Who needs a key to use a bathroom? That feels cruel. What if it's truly an emergency, and not a fib like I told Impatient Woman to get into the bathroom lobby? They'd be out of luck.

Quickly, I make my way toward the café. Why is it that once you decide you have to go, your brain doesn't let you stop thinking about how badly you have to go?

I hasten my steps.

Not too much farther.

The bathroom.

Something itches at the back of my brain.

The locked bathroom at the House of Ministries.

What if *that* is the key I get? Stealing a key to the restroom is more likely to go unnoticed than if I try to steal a key to the entire building. Once I have the key, I'll slip in first. Then—one at a time—throughout the day—I'll let everyone else into the women's restroom. All ten of us. The boys may need to wear disguises to look like girls? We'll hide in the stalls until the building closes. When night falls, we'll go to the roof. We'll escape.

I'm so excited I might pee myself.

CHAPTER 33

In the morning, I stare at the crack beneath my apartment door.

Mama has left for work already. After being asked to leave early on Monday and having off yesterday, she said she was antsy to get back to the lab.

I'm glad Mama likes her work.

She's been fortunate.

If only there was a guarantee I'd like my future job, too. But there isn't.

I think of Monika, stuck in a job she hates.

Where *is* Monika?

I'm desperate for a response from her. Last night, Katarina and I snuck up to Katarina's rooftop again. Even knowing the rope would be too heavy on the arrow, we had to confirm it. Too heavy.

The clock begins to chime the first of seven *dong*s.

If Monika is going to respond to my note from yesterday, now would be the time.

Come on.

Come on.

Footsteps!

A letter slides under the door. Then I watch as something else is shoved underneath in a big lump. Floss? No, it's thicker.

I grab Monika's note.

There's plenty of fishing line here.

I bunch it in my hand. It weights practically nothing. Yes, this could work.

That night, I pause outside Mama's bedroom door. She's breathing evenly, soundly. I tiptoe down the hallway, stepping to the right to avoid a noisy creak in the floor.

Even after successfully sneaking out last night, my heart is beating wildly.

Outside, I quickly run from each streetlamp's halo of light to the next. A dog barks, and I jump. Katarina is waiting at the door.

We exchange a secretive grin; then we climb the stairs to her roof.

The bird screeches upon our arrival.

I shush it.

"I've got the fishing line," I say, holding it up. The moon is still large, only just beginning to wane, and the roof is bright. The fishing line itself glows in the night, making it appear almost magical. I get to work taping it to the arrow.

I've been giddy all day, waiting for this moment.

We're both smiling when I hand back the arrow.

She does her thing, her movements practiced now as she readies the arrow on the bow. I'm still so impressed with how quickly she picked up archery. After the Great Nose Bleed of 1970, when Katarina got hit in the face by a soccer ball, we both wrote off sports. But maybe we're more athletic than we realized. Or Katarina, at least.

The bowstring is pressed against her face. She barely moves her lips when she says, "I'm nervous. Count me down from three."

The cable didn't work. The rope didn't work. Easter is in only four days. The fishing line *has* to work.

I lick my chapped lips. Katarina repositions her feet, making sure her stance is perfect, then slightly shifts the bowstring so it's at the corner of her mouth. "Here we go, Katy," I whisper. "You've got this. Three, two, one . . ."

She releases the arrow.

It flies!

The roof is long, Katarina's building touching the one next to it and sharing a roof.

I chase after the arrow, mentally counting as I go. Five, ten, fifteen, twenty.

I proclaim, "Katy, we're doing it! *You're* doing it!" I study her face in the moonlight. "Wait, why aren't you excited?"

"It's not far enough. We need more than thirty."

I run back to her with the arrow and shake her shoulder. "*That* was your first time with the fishing line. Look what you just did. Now that we know the fishing line is light enough, you just need to practice."

"The weight did make it feel different."

"See!" I say.

The stupid bird screeches, and we both ignore it, Katarina saying, "I want to try again."

I stand back and let Katy do her thing. The arrow doesn't go any farther, but it also doesn't go any shorter of a distance either.

"Again," she says, determined.

I run to retrieve the arrow for her. I imagine Escape Night. Katarina will shoot the arrow with the fishing line. It'll soar over the wall. Ava will retrieve the arrow and reel in the fishing line. We'll already have the fishing line attached to the sturdier cable. Ava will pull in the line until she gets to the cable. She'll attach it on her side. We'll zip across, one after another.

Katarina smiles and nocks the arrow for her next shot.

CHAPTER 34

All that remains is the key.

It's the final piece of the puzzle, and a huge one.

In the morning, I write back to Monika with a single non-incriminating word: *Works!*

Before I leave for school, I set my tape trap.

At the corner, I wait for Katarina to discuss Escape Night on the way to school.

What a weird routine I have now. But hopefully not for much longer.

"I'm not going to practice with Anton this afternoon."

My head whips toward her. "What?"

"I'll practice on the roof tonight." She yawns. "But I *only* want to practice with the fishing line. I need to perfect that and using an arrow without the fishing line will only mess me up."

"But what about Anton?"

She smiles. "Suddenly you care about Anton now?"

"I care about you. You won't have that time with him."

"Who said that? We're still going to hang out."

My best friend really likes him. I may not know what that feels like, liking a boy, but it's easy to tell it makes her happy. What *that* does is make me feel horrible I said he couldn't escape with us—if he even *wants* to. I take a deep breath. "Do you think Anton would want to go, too?"

Katarina stops walking. She lays a hand on my arm. "I get why you said he can't come, Soph. I was mad at first, but I get it. It's not like we could kidnap Anton away from his parents. They're a package deal. I also know now he's got a big family. Two brothers and a baby sister."

The math is easy. That would've meant adding six people to our original ten. *And* one of those would be a baby that we'd have to keep quiet while hiding in bathroom stalls.

"It sucks," she goes on. "I'm going to miss him. But I don't know, once I'm over there, maybe I can think of a way to help him and his family get over, too."

"You've got a big heart, Katy."

She smiles. "Thanks, Soph. But of course, my saving

Anton is dependent on you getting that key so *we* can get out of here first."

I groan. "Don't remind me."

"You can do it."

It's the same thing I told Katarina about shooting the bow and arrow. She can do that now. And I love that she believes in me, too. I can do this.

I may even have an idea. I say, "Herr Becker left his office once before when I was there, but only for a second. What if I could get him to leave for longer?"

"And search for a bathroom key in his office?"

I shrug but follow it with a serious nod. "Everyone's got to go."

"I guess. But we'd be assuming they use the same bathroom key for the men's and women's rooms."

I nod more excitably. "They do, actually! I saw one of the secretaries use her key to let a man into the restrooms once. I'm going to hypothesize that the same key is used for *all* the restrooms on *all* the floors."

"I support that hypothesis."

"Great," I say, "because I'm going to need your help."

Katarina wiggles her fingers in a *bring it on* gesture. I can't help laughing. We've come a long way from the two girls who once only joked about shooting ourselves over the Wall in a rocket. We're brave.

But being brave doesn't make me any less scared that our plan could fail. Still we have to try. "Okay, here's what we're going to do."

I am brave, I remind myself as I take a seat across from Herr Becker.

It's hard to believe *tomorrow* is Easter.

My eyes drop to where I know his desk drawer is, to where I hope a bathroom key is. From my side of the desk, all I can see is his desktop, though. It's pristine, everything in its place.

"So nice to see you again, Sophie."

"You too," I lie.

He spreads his hands apart, palms up. "What do you have for me today?"

I picture Katarina running down the sidewalk. She watched me go into the House of Ministries; then she took off. I bet she's nearly at the public pay phone.

"About Monika?" I ask him. I already have something prepared to say, but I'm stalling.

"Is there anyone else you'd like to talk about? Perhaps your good friend Katarina?"

I suck in a breath. "Katarina?"

"She seems to have taken up a hobby in archery." He laughs. "At first I thought both of you had, but it appears you don't have a knack for the sport. Katarina, however"—he whistles—"she's gotten quite good. Your school doesn't have a girls' team. That makes me wonder why Katarina is putting in such an effort. Until the past two days, that is. She suddenly stopped practicing. That's also curious, is it not?"

I despise this man.

I despise how he watches me and everyone I care about.

"She likes a boy. He's an archer," I say sharply, maybe too sharply. "She was afraid to talk to him at first, so I went, too. But as you said, I'm not any good at it. But now that she knows he likes her back, they did something different the past two days. Maybe they saw a movie? I don't know. Maybe you could tell me?"

Herr Becker stares at me. His nostrils flare.

I definitely took it too far.

I bite the inside of my cheek.

Just then, there's a knock at his office door.

He doesn't answer.

There's another knock. It's louder, but hurried, like Nasal Woman is nervous to interrupt.

I will him to answer her.

"What?" he barks.

Nasal Woman timidly pokes her head into the room. "I have someone on the phone who says she must talk to you right away."

"Who?" Herr Becker snaps.

"She said she's one of your informants?"

Herr Becker lets out a slow, controlled breath.

Nasal Woman quickly adds, "I didn't want to transfer it without asking first since you have a guest."

Herr Becker glares at me, as if he thinks I'm the reason why there's a phone call interrupting our meeting. He'd be right. I hide a grin.

He pushes back his chair, the legs angrily scraping against the floor. Herr Becker storms out of the room. But I can also see the intrigue on his face as he rubs his chin. Is he trying to figure out which informant could be calling?

Nasal Woman's desk is in an open area at the end of the hall.

It won't take Herr Becker long to get there and to get back.

Hopefully, Katarina can keep him on the phone long enough.

Nasal Woman looks hesitant to leave me sitting alone in Herr Becker's office. She glances down the hall, deciding between me and Herr Becker.

I smile sweetly.

She hurries after her boss.

In a heartbeat, I'm on my feet. The door to Herr Becker's office is still open. If anyone walks by, they'll see me snooping. But Katarina said we have to take chances.

She's currently spouting the lie of her life—that she was at a café and heard a group of people planning an escape.

I have to risk getting caught stealing a key.

It feels weird to be on Herr Becker's side of the desk, but it's a fleeting thought. I rip open one of his desk drawers, the exact one where I saw him retrieve the key for the filing cabinet. I see *that* key, but no others.

There are three other drawers. Time is ticking. I begin opening, searching, and closing.

No!

Does this man never use the bathroom?

I bet he expects Nasal Woman to let him in. I wouldn't be surprised. He's demanding. Unfair.

He's the worst.

I slam the last drawer, cringing at the *bang*, and peer at the doorway. No one is there. I hope no one comes to investigate the noise. I'm about to return to my seat, a big fat failure, when my gaze falls on the filing cabinets.

Hadn't I wanted to steal my files?

It's risky. He could notice before we escape. But this could be my only chance at the files.

I take the key from the first drawer and go to the cabinet on the far right. It's where Monika's file was. I fumble with the key but finally unlock the drawer. It's a slew of names that begin with *V*. Monika's last name is Voigt.

There are three drawers below this one. I bet the Zs are in one of those. That's where the files on Mama and me will be.

But first, Monika's.

I begin thumbing through the files.

Yes!

Found it.

Voigt, Monika.

I begin to pull it out, planning to hide it under my shirt, when my eye falls on another file name. *Volker, Anton.*

No!

Is Anton under suspicion, too? Is he an informant like me?

Whatever he is, there's a file with his name on it. That's not good.

Originally, I wanted to steal my file, Mama's, and Monika's. I wanted to rip up the contract I signed with Herr Becker to shreds. But if I steal our files and also Anton's—and if Herr Becker realizes which files were stolen together—that will put suspicion on Anton. A lot of it.

I hear a cough from the hallway.

I jump.

I have a decision to make, and quick!

CHAPTER 35

I rip Anton's file from the cabinet.

I shove it under my shirt and zip my jacket, which will help hide the shape of the folder.

Herr Becker will be here soon.

Even though I can't take my file, I can look in it. I can see if there's any evidence that Herr Becker knows about tomorrow's visit. Does he have a copy of the letter Ava mailed to me?

I begin to reach for the handle of another drawer, but his voice stops me. My hand hovers in midair.

Herr Becker is coming back down the hallway.

As quickly and quietly as possible I tiptoe to his desk. I put the key back *exactly* as I found it. He'd notice otherwise. I know it.

My butt is barely in the visitor chair when Herr Becker tramps back into his office.

I'm sitting ramrod straight; I have to. Anton's file doesn't allow me to slouch even a little bit. I pray he can't see the outline of it beneath my jacket.

"I apologize for the interruption," Herr Becker says.

"It's okay."

I hope he dismisses me now.

"Where were we?" he asks.

I keep my mouth shut.

"Monika. Do you have anything to report?"

I give him my rehearsed line, another one that won't get Monika or anyone in trouble. But I don't think Herr Becker is even listening. He has something he wants to say—and he says it: "Monika purchased fishing line earlier this week. Do you have any idea why?"

I was not expecting this. All I can do is repeat him. "She purchased fishing line earlier this week?"

"That's what I said. Do you have any idea why?"

"Um," I begin. But I can't think of anything to say. All my brain can think is: *He knows! He's baiting me.*

I dig my thumbnail into my palm. I concentrate on the sharp pain. A lie filters into my head. "A new hobby? Kind of like how Katarina learned archery for a boy at school."

"Are you telling me Monika has become particularly close with a man in her new circle of friends? An older man?"

The question feels like a trap. And then I want to smack myself upside the head. I know why he's asking. Before, I told him that an older man Monika may know has been scheming an escape.

My mouth is suddenly bone dry. "I can find out," I struggle to say.

"You do that, Sophie. And call me as soon as you know. This cannot wait a week. Understood?"

"Yes, sir," I manage, and I stand to leave, discreetly pressing my arm across my stomach so Anton's file doesn't fall free. My legs can barely hold me.

"Sophie?"

My name sounds like a gunshot to my ears.

"Yes?"

He gives me a type of grin only a villain can. All teeth. Too wide. "Enjoy the rest of your weekend."

As soon as I'm in the hallway and out of Herr Becker's line of sight, I shudder.

Nasal Woman is leading me out of the building.

I press harder against my stomach, keeping the file in place.

It's a small consolation. I didn't get the key. Without it, the entire plan is off. And more than ever, we need to get out of here. I just messed up. Big-time. I can't believe I made up a fake crush that puts very real speculation on Monika.

But I can't focus on that right now. I breathe out a calming breath. Katarina and I came up with a backup plan. Nasal Woman directs me into the lobby, and I say, "Excuse me, I need to use the restroom."

She checks her watch.

I shift my weight from side to side while holding out my hand for the key.

But instead of putting the key into my palm like Katarina and I hoped she would, Nasal Woman brushes past me. Her heels *click-clack* toward the lobby. "You're in a hurry, I see," I say. "Why don't I just lock up behind me when I'm done and leave the key with the front desk?"

I smile.

She shakes her head. "No need, the door will lock behind you when you leave. Go straight out of the building, understood?"

"But . . ." I begin to say. I have no clue how to finish my sentence.

Nasal Woman opens the door for me. "In or out."

I walk into the bathroom like I'm walking the plank and *all* my planning is about to sink with me.

The door closes at my heels.

This is horrible.

Plan B has also failed. We don't have a plan C.

There are no windows in here to prop open. There are only five stalls. Five sinks. It would've been a great hiding spot. But no, I couldn't get the key we needed.

Escape Night is off, and all because of me.

CHAPTER 36

Katarina recognizes the failure on my face as soon as I round the corner to our street.

She's waiting outside my apartment building, her hands pressed together in front of her chest. "No," she says. "You couldn't get it."

My shoulders rise, fall. Tears spring to my eyes.

Before I know it, Katarina's arms are around me. "It's okay. We'll figure out something else. We always do. We managed to get the wheel to stay on the go-cart, remember?"

I do. We eventually flew safely and swiftly down the hill. The stakes this time are greater than a skinned knee, though. At least I was able to help Anton. I say, "I have something for you I think you'll like. I can't give it to you out here, though."

"What—"

"Girls?"

I turn to find Mama wheeling toward us.

"Hi, Mama," I say.

"Hello, Angelika," Katarina says. Mama has always insisted Katarina call her by her first name. Maybe because our last name is fake. My eyes begin to tear again, thinking we were so close to getting to the West and taking the name Mama had while growing up. I don't even know what that name is. But I want it so badly right now. My tears overflow.

Mama is out of her chair in a heartbeat. I didn't know she could stand that quickly. "Darling?" she says. "What is it? I'm here. Talk to me."

Talk to her.

I don't even know if it's worth telling her about Escape Night now. The plan was to finalize everything with Ava tomorrow. But if I don't have the key to get us all into the building, what's the point? Mama will just be furious at me for all the risks I've taken lately.

One of those risks is literally hiding beneath my jacket and shirt.

"I think we should tell her, Soph."

"Tell me what?" Mama says. "Girls, whatever it is, I promise to listen. Let's go inside."

"All right," I say in a small voice. "But I'm not sure I should tell you inside in case they're listening."

"Who? Our neighbors?"

"No," I say, "the Stasi."

Mama's face turns as white as a ghost, and she slowly lowers herself again to her chair. "Tell me everything."

Before I can tell Mama a single thing inside, she sweeps our apartment for any listening bugs. She did this before but didn't seem like she had a clue what she was looking for. Now she does. I watch in awe as she twists the radio dial to a "quiet" frequency and then wheels around the apartment, holding the small hand-held radio up to lamps and such.

While Mama is doing that, I pull the file from beneath my shirt and silently hand it to Katarina.

Her eyes are big as saucers when she sees the name.

But when we open it, we receive a second surprise. It's not our Anton who the file is about. He's named after his papa—and that's whose file I took. Still, Katarina throws her arms around me and whispers, "Thank you," into my ear. We both know that Anton's father getting in trouble could mean trouble for the entire family. By getting rid of this file, we erased everything the Stasi has on his family.

I clench my fist, this moment inspiring me. We did something. We did something really good. I'd like to do something like that again.

"All done," Mama says. "If there was something here, we'd hear a high-pitched squeal."

Even so, there's still the neighbors to consider overhearing us, and Mama tunes the radio to a music station, raises the volume, puts the radio on the coffee table between the three of us, and says, "Start talking, darlings."

I begin at Monika's arrest. I tell her how that same morning Herr Becker contacted me. I confess how I signed an agreement to spy for him. I tell her why I agreed to it—to first save her, but also now to save Monika.

Mama has to look away when I tell her that. But she doesn't interrupt. Wordlessly, she motions for me to keep going.

I confess how Katarina and I have dreamed of silly ways to escape for years. Katarina explains how we both want more than the life the East can give us. I describe the roof at the House of Ministries and how it cuts into the death strip. We walk her through our plans, how we want to zip-line across on a cable and how Katarina will first shoot a fishing line across so we can attach the cable. I emphasize how hard she practiced and confess that we've been sneaking up to her roof every night to continue practicing.

The whole time, Katarina and I hold hands. She knows just as well as I do about my mama's volcanic emotions. I am sure she'll burst soon, unable to contain how angry she is at me.

Before she can, I press on. I still have to tell her about the real reason our family is coming tomorrow. Mama holds a hand over her mouth.

"Ava is in on this, too?" Mama says, almost to herself. "You running into her wasn't a mistake?"

"Not the second time," I confess.

"Unbelievable," Mama says.

Her face is so hard to read, her emotions still beneath the surface. But I think there's a hint of intrigue in how her right eyebrow is slightly raised.

"Where are you two now with this plan of yours?"

I sigh. "I couldn't get the key to the bathroom. So I guess nowhere. The idea was that we'd all sneak into the building throughout the day. I'd go first and then let everyone into the bathroom. We'd all hide until the building closed for the night. All we'd have to do then was get to the roof. We were going to pick a day with Ava tomorrow for the escape. But without the key . . ."

I feel exhausted and don't finish. I don't want to say it out loud again that I've failed.

Mama is silent. She then begins to wheel away from us.

She goes to the end of the hallway and stares at nothing. A crack on the wall perhaps?

She's thinking.

She thinks for what feels like forever. I watch as she licks her lips, runs a hand over her hair, stares off at the distance. Any moment I'm expecting her to come back and yell at us.

When she does begin to return, I hold my breath. Katarina's chest isn't moving either.

"Girls, thank you for telling me all that. *Finally.*"

She puts a stern emphasis on that last word, and I find myself shrinking at her tone.

"I'm sorry, Mama. I didn't want to tell you any of this until I was sure we could pull it off."

"You got close, girls. Really close."

Now is when she'll let us have it. I'll be grounded.

She'll tell Katarina's mama. Katy will be grounded.

Except, Mama doesn't reprimand us. She wrings her hands together, then gives a hard squeeze, like a punctuation to a difficult decision. She says, "You two remind me a lot of myself as a young woman. I made hard choices for what I believed in, too. And I hid it from the people I loved to protect them." Mama shakes her head. "I can't believe you've been doing all this to protect me from the Stasi. It's my job to protect *you*. To help you."

I remember how Mama helped a resistance group in the Second World War. Mama can relate. I let my shoulders relax a tiny bit. "So you're not mad?"

"Oh, I'm furious that you two have been lying and running around like you're invincible. And an informant? Sophie." Mama takes the biggest gulp of air I've ever seen her take. She then cups my cheek. "Everything you've done is dangerous. Extremely dangerous. But I've always wanted more than *this* life for you, especially since it's all my fault we're here."

"Mama—"

She holds up a hand to stop me. "Your plan is incredibly intelligent, girls. It's also very time sensitive with the family coming tomorrow. We may not get another chance to talk openly with them like this. That's why I'm not going to stop you. I'm going to help you. We're going to get that key together, and we're going to escape."

CHAPTER 37

Katarina and I both have our mouths open wide enough to catch flies.

Mama wants to help us?

She wants to go through with Escape Night?

I expected smoke to pour out of her ears when I told her I was a spy.

But escaping this life is more important, maybe *especially* now that she knows Herr Becker has made me his informant.

"Now," she says, "we don't have much time. We need to communicate the plan to everyone tomorrow," she stresses again. "That means we need to get the key today. Right now. After we have the key, I don't think we should share it. I want to duplicate it."

Before my eyes, Mama has transformed into a comic book superhero. We have comic books here, but just like our television shows, I've heard they aren't as good as the ones the West has. Soon, I'll see it all with my own eyes.

A giddiness fills me.

"You want to make more keys?"

Mama nods. "Yes, we should each have one. Otherwise, knocking on the bathroom door to be let in could draw extra attention. We can't have that. We also will need to plan our arrivals at times when the lobby has an influx of people. First thing in the morning. Leaving for lunch. Returning from lunch. End of day."

Katarina's mouth still hangs open. It makes me giggle. Mine would be, too, if I didn't have questions to ask. "How are we going to make keys?"

Mama smiles. It's a conspiratorial-like smile, like she's a cat about to get a bird. "We're going to create a casting. The party made a mistake the day they assigned me a job in a lab."

Mama winks. Unlike Katarina and me, she can actually do it.

Katarina clasps her hands together excitedly.

My heart soars. Escape Night is back on.

I may be nearly thirteen, but I jump around the apartment as Mama spouts off instructions.

"I need a small box. Two of them."

"Like a shoebox?" I say.

"Too big," Mama replies.

"A tuna can," Katarina suggests.

"Perfect, Katy."

We run toward the kitchen, grab two cans off the shelf, and empty them. There's no getting rid of the smell. Mama says that's okay.

"Now we need a soft material. You don't have any clay, do you, Soph?" Mama asks me.

I shake my head.

So does Katarina.

"That's okay. We have silicone at the lab. I'll need zinc from there, too, anyway." Mama pauses. Thinks. "I'll go to the lab. I'll get the key. Then I'll be back. You two stay here."

"What? No, Mama. We want to come. We want to help get the key."

Mama shakes her head. "I'm the parent. If Katarina's parents knew I let her be involved . . ."

"She's already involved, Mama. So am I. We can help. Up until now, we've done everything ourselves."

Under her breath, Mama says, "That's the problem."

I smile at that. We've done *a lot*.

"Fine, you can come. But I want you to stay outside. You don't go near either building."

It's a start.

Katarina and I grab our coats. My roll of transparent tape is in my pocket. In the hallway, I pause to set my tape trap.

Mama watches. This time it's her mouth hanging open. She whispers, "Sophie, the fact you think to do that is both very smart and very scary. Once you're out of this confined world, you're going to make a big difference in the real world. I know it. You both are."

Pride at Mama's words nearly has me floating down the hallway.

Once we're at Mama's work, she insists again we wait outside. She's not supposed to be there right now, and it'd look even stranger if she brings in two kids with her. Luckily, she has what she needs in no time. We duck into an alley, which can't look anything but suspicious. But we're also short on options. "Hold these," she says to us, referring to the tuna cans. She quickly fills them with the silicone. "I'll press the key into these," she explains as she hides them behind her in her wheelchair.

I can't help but think it again. My mama could be a superhero.

Next, we're outside the House of Ministries. "So what are you going to do?" I ask her as we approach.

"I plan to ask the man at the front desk for the bathroom key."

It's simple. But if I know anything, it's that nothing ever goes as planned. I don't object to her plan, though. Katarina and I go inside a bus stop shelter and settle onto a bench. I watch her go toward the building; then I whisper to Katarina, "If she's not back in five minutes, I'm going in. I have an idea."

I shrug off my coat.

Casually, I look around. There doesn't seem to be anyone secretly watching us. It'd be a miracle if no one followed us today. But miracles happen.

I'm afraid Mama getting the key won't be one of them.

I don't know if it's been five minutes. To me, it's been long enough.

"Be right back," I say to Katarina. "If the bus comes, get on it and go to my apartment."

I jog toward the building.

Once I'm inside, I scan the lobby. Mama is still at the front desk. She's in her wheelchair, off to the side of the desk, and gesturing toward the man.

"Excuse me," I say, walking up.

They both stop and look at me. There's annoyance on the man's face. Mama's shows anger.

The man ignores me and turns back to Mama. "Like I said, the bathroom is only for employees or guests of the building."

"Excuse me," I say again. "I was here earlier and—"

"Sir," Mama interrupts, "like I was saying, it's an emergency. I had some bad tuna for lunch," Mama says and makes a face like she *really* needs to use the restroom.

The man's nose twitches. He's *got* to be able to smell the tuna. I sure can.

Mama repositions in her chair.

The man looks at me. "Are you still here? What do you want, kid?"

"I was here earlier, and I forgot my coat. I wanted to see if anyone turned it in."

"Uh-oh," Mama says then. She clutches at her stomach.

The man looks between us. He's overwhelmed. His eyes are big. I hope he's too overwhelmed, in fact, to tell that Mama and I look alike. We're a team.

"No," he says to me. "No coat."

"Are you sure?" I ask just as Mama says, "I don't think I can hold it much longer."

The man throws up his hands.

"Here," he says to Mama, handing her the bathroom key. "Bring it right back. And you," he says to me, "there's no coat. Now leave. I have work to do."

Mama wastes no time snatching the key, dropping it into her lap, and moving toward the bathroom.

I let out an aggravated sigh but also don't waste any time leaving the desk.

The man looks relieved to be rid of us both.

I hurry back to Katarina at the bus stop, just as a bus is approaching. "Let's take it," I say. "I don't want us to be seen leaving with my mama."

"Did she get it?" Katarina whispers.

I grin so wide there's no need to answer the question.

I picture Mama in the bathroom, pressing the key into the tuna tins. When she carefully removes the key, impressions will be left behind in the silicone. From that, we'll make a key—again and again and again. Nothing can stop us now.

CHAPTER 38

Back at my apartment, I turn on both the oven and the stove. I put a pan on top. I'll get it ready for Mama. She said she'll need to melt the zinc and bake the silicone.

I work in such a hurry that I don't realize Katarina looks nervous.

"What's wrong?" I ask her.

"What if my parents say no?"

"They can't."

Katarina slumps down into a kitchen chair. "They can. They're my parents."

I pull out the chair across from her. "My mama will talk to them. If she's on board, she can get them on board, too."

"My parents weren't in a resistance like she was. They may not think the same way."

"My mama will talk to them." I reach across the table and squeeze her hand. "It'll be okay."

"It better be. *I'm* the one who is supposed to shoot the arrow."

I'm leaning forward. I had to stretch to reach her hand. I'm still as a statue now. "I didn't think about that."

"Yeah . . ."

Just then, the door rattles and Mama comes in.

She points to the top of the door, to where the tape was. She mouths, *The tape?*

"It was still there," I answer.

"Good, I don't need to sweep again. But, Sophie . . . Sophie, I thought I was clear about staying outside."

"You were. But you needed me. I helped."

Mama closes her eyes as she takes a very deep breath. "We have the key impression, that's what's important right now." When Mama opens her eyes, she means business. A woman on a mission. "Let's get started."

She smiles at me when she sees I already have the pot heating. She first creates air funnels in the silicone. "This'll allow the heat to escape." She then places the zinc in the pot. Slowly it melts and melts until it's no longer a solid but a liquid.

Mama rises from her wheelchair for the next part. "Stand back, girls." She carefully pours the casting material into the key impressions she made in the silicone. "We'll bake these," she tells us. "Once they're hardened, we'll carefully remove our new key from the mold and clean it up. Voilà! We'll have an identical key."

"And repeat," I say, smiling.

"And repeat. This is kind of what I did during the war. We duplicated leaflets to distribute throughout Germany."

Mama looks lost in her thoughts for a moment. Back then, it sounds like she helped lots of people. Now the two of us have to start by helping ourselves.

That night, Mama wants to join us on the roof while Katarina practices.

We've gotten smart and now bring a sheet to drape over the large birdcage. The creepy bird stays quiet if it can't see us.

Mama insists she climb the staircase on her own. She'll need to do the same on Escape Night.

It takes a long, long time.

It's Mama's left side of her body that was damaged most by her polio, and she leans heavily on her right side. Every time I try to help her, she grunts at me and I pull my hand back.

Finally, we reach the roof. The moon is still waning, casting a soft glow.

Katarina and I retrieve her bow and our supplies from our hiding spot behind the birdcage. We quickly hide the bird, too.

Confidently, Katarina gets her body into position, nocks the arrow, lines up her shot, and releases the arrow.

We have the science figured perfectly for the arc and trajectory. We've practiced pulling the fishing line, which will be attached to the cable. What we haven't practiced is riding the actual zip line. But over the past few nights on the roof, I've fashioned the handlebar, the purse strap, and the swing seat into one piece. I knotted a rope to it so that it can be pulled back up the zip line.

I study our operation.

"Unbelievable," Mama whispers.

When Katarina takes a break, I ask her if she spoke to her parents yet.

"They didn't say no. They also didn't say yes. My poor mama looked like she was going to faint, actually. My papa said they'll sleep on it."

"Why doesn't your family join ours for Easter dinner tomorrow? I'll talk it out with your parents."

Katarina nods. She runs a hand down the bow. "Soph, even if my parents say no, I'm still going to the roof. I'll shoot the bow for you."

"You're coming," I insist. "I'm not leaving you here. This is our plan. You are my best friend." My voice quakes on those last words.

Mama puts a hand on each of our shoulders. "Tomorrow, girls. Let's leave this for tomorrow."

Tomorrow comes.

The day feels heavy.

It's raining.

There's a chill in the air, even inside.

I realize I never watered the bluestar plant I brought to my room. It's not looking so good. But there are other things on my mind. A lot of them, including the fact I need to update Monika. It'll be the very last time I take the risk of writing her. I quickly scribble a note to slide under her door.

Plan is on!

I also tell her to come over for dinner with her family so that everyone can get their key and we can go over the final plan.

After slipping the note under her door, I skip back to my own.

This doesn't feel like real life.

Today I am seeing Ava again.

Today the rest of the family I've never met is coming here.

Today Mama will see her family for the first time in twelve years.

Today we'll finalize Escape Night.

And Katarina *will* be coming. *She's coming.* Mama will persuade Katarina's parents to leave the East.

I reenter the apartment to find Mama in a flurry of motion. She's cleaning. She's organizing. She has stuff on the stove. She has recipes out on the table. I rescue the pillow she's overfluffing. "Today's going to be perfect, Mama."

She snorts. "It's just a big day, that's all, darling."

If she wasn't already sitting, she looks like she'd want to, judging by the long expression she's wearing.

"What's wrong?" I ask her.

"Part of me is afraid they'll all be upset with me. I chased after your father. I got us stuck here. Then I purposely hid us from them, from everyone. I can't believe it's been over a decade. They've missed so much of your life."

"A life that will continue with them. That's all that matters. Come on," I say, "let's finish getting ready."

Before I know it, there's a knock at the door.

Mama and I lock eyes.

They're here. Or we assume it's them. I only wonder for a moment. The people on the other side of the door are sobbing. It can't be anyone else but our long-lost family.

CHAPTER 39

Mama stands from her chair, bracing herself with a hand on the wheelchair's armrest before she fully lets go. She's nervous about how they are going to react. So am I, but for different reasons. What if they don't like me? What if they've dreamed of who I'd be for the past twelve years, and I don't live up to it?

Mama says in a soft voice, "Go on, Sophie."

I open the door.

A woman gasps.

Mama gasps.

Ava barrels into me.

I'm laughing. I'm crying.

Before I know it, my Aunt Brigitte is hugging me next. "Sophie, oh, Sophie. Dear Sophie. It's really you. I've dreamed of this day for so long." Aunt Brigitte holds me at arm's length, really looking at me with her bright blue eyes. "I've dreamed of you, and here you are, exactly as you're meant to be." A warmth fills me as her gaze rises, meeting Mama's. "Angelika," she whispers. I step aside, and the two sisters slowly approach each other. Aunt Brigitte runs the last few steps, enveloping Mama in a hug.

I look at the rest of my family. My uncle is standing, an arm around his other two daughters . . . my other two cousins, Annett and Erika. And next to them: my grandfather. His eyes are so blurry with tears I wonder if he can see a thing. Though it'd be hard to miss the many plants Mama bought just for him.

"Grandpa?" I say in a small voice.

He opens his mouth, but no words come out. He only motions for me to come to him. He looks frail, his hair completely gray. His eyes are a pale blue, but I can tell they were once as vibrant as Aunt Brigitte's. With a strength I don't expect, he pulls me the last step toward him. With his other hand, he pulls in Annett and Erika. Erika grabs Ava. For the first time, he has an arm around *all* his grandchildren. "My flowers," he whispers. "My petunia," he says louder, and Mama joins us in our hug.

Aunt Brigitte claps her hands. She sniffles. Her cheeks are red from her reunion with Mama. My uncle

Rolf has an arm around her. She shakes out her hands, like she's trying to shake out the excess emotion. "Okay, everyone. First, we eat. Then, we scheme. Never again will our family be apart."

"You seriously don't have bananas?" Ava asks Katarina and me.

Katarina arrived with her parents and brother not long ago. We've eaten and the grown-ups are in the kitchen now, talking. Persuading. Convincing. Inspiring. The radio is turned up so loud it's almost hard to hear my cousins, who are sitting right next to me.

"I've had bananas before," I say. "But we don't get them often. You can always tell when the store gets them in because the line is longer than usual."

"And it's usually long to begin with," Katarina stresses.

"Well, soon you can have a banana every day if you want," Erika says with a smile. "You'll have so many just the idea of them will make you feel like throwing up."

I'm not sure I'd want that. But I'm excited about the idea of getting sick of bananas.

"Have any of us stopped smiling?" Annett asks. She's my oldest cousin, nearly seventeen. She's the one named after my grandmother. "I still can't believe how much you and Ava look alike."

"Like grandma," Ava says.

"She'd like knowing you're together," Annett says. "If you two schemed up all this after seeing each other for all of thirty seconds, I can only imagine what you'll get into back home."

"The three of us," I say, including Katarina. She's staring into the kitchen at her parents. They still haven't said if they are coming or not. I feel bad for letting my excitement about being in the West bubble over when Katarina still doesn't know if she's coming.

"Lord help us," Annett says jokingly. "The three of you will start your own invention company."

"I like the sound of that!"

"Me too," Katarina begins, but then goes silent. Her parents are in the doorway to the living room. Katarina is looking with such hope at her parents that I think she may burst. Her mama is crying, from the idea of leaving her home or from being about to disappoint her daughter, I'm not sure which. She's also wringing her hands. My attention is pulled there. And in her hands, I see something.

A key.

I elbow Katarina. Her mama wouldn't have a key if she's not coming.

Katarina is coming!

She runs to them, her foot catching on the rug, and she falls into her papa's arms.

We all laugh. With our laughter and the music, I almost miss the knock on the door.

Now's the time when Herr Becker will show up. Things are too good. We're too happy. I hesitate before turning the knob, launching myself at Monika when I see it's only her. "You're here!"

Instantly, something feels wrong. She's hugging me back, but it's more like she's holding me up instead of embracing me. Monika also isn't saying a thing. I pull away. "Where are your parents? Your brother?"

She eases the door closed behind her. "They aren't coming. My father said he can't leave his practice and his patients. He has people who depend on him, and he refuses to abandon them. My mama and my brother won't go unless my father does."

"And you?" I say, even though her expression reveals the truth. She's not coming. Monika . . . who I've known since I was a little girl, who dreamed with me, who invented with me, who took care of me . . . isn't coming with me. This isn't how I pictured it. This isn't how Escape Night is supposed to go.

"Sophie," Monika whispers. Her eyes flick behind me, they dart to my face, but then away from me again.

Monika seems nervous.

Mama is behind me then. "Monika?" she asks.

Monika has no choice but to look at us.

"What is it?" I press. There's something she's not telling us.

Monika swallows roughly. Her mouth opens, but no words come out. Finally, she says, "They know about the escape."

CHAPTER 40

They know about the escape.

"Who?" Mama demands. "Who knows?"

Herr Becker, I think.

Surprising me, Monika says, "My friends." She's quick to add, "After I told them, they said they wanted to come, too. But I told them they couldn't. It's too many people. I won't go either, to make sure someone is there to stop them if they try to get in the building."

Monika told her friends? The betrayal I feel nearly bends me in half. I could vomit in the new plant by the door. "But we pinkie-swore."

Monika whispers, "I know. I'm so sorry, Sophie. I was frustrated with my job. Then I was boasting about your plan."

"We pinkie-swore," I repeat. "You know how serious this is. How dangerous this is. How could you tell anyone?"

Mama wraps an arm around me. She's trembling. I'm trembling, too. I feel the eyes of my family on us. No one utters a word.

"Do you trust them?" Mama asks.

It's the delay in Monika's response that has Mama shaking her head. It's so hard to know who you can and cannot trust in this world. And even if you think you can trust someone, sometimes they break your heart.

Mama reaches around Monika to open the door, but Monika holds out a hand to stop her. "I won't let them get in the way," Monika pleads. "They don't know when."

I question, "But you told them where and how?"

Monika's nod is barely there. So is my voice as I say, "Then you aren't welcome here."

I don't want to physically force Monika to leave, and I'm relieved when she goes on her own. Mama's gait back toward our family is unsteady. There are tears in everyone's eyes.

"What do we do?" Aunt Brigitte asks.

"You all need to leave. *Now*," Mama says.

Katarina begins crying. Or maybe it's Ava. I'm not sure. I'm staring at Mama. I've never seen her so scared. But I also know how brave she can be. Lately, I've seen how brave I can be. I'm named after a war hero. My father was relentless for what he believed in. I've learned that things go wrong, but you can't give up. I never knew my dad, but he's still a part of me. I have a feeling he'd believe in me, no matter what. I need to believe in me, too. I need to be relentless. I need to believe in what Katarina and I have planned and replanned.

"We're still doing it," I say.

Mama's eyes scrunch together in a melting pot of confusion, anger, and fear. "Of course we're not."

"We're escaping," I insist. "I'm not throwing away this opportunity. You heard her . . ." I mean Monika, but it hurts to say her name. "They don't know when we're going. They don't have all that we have." The keys. The bow and arrow. The fishing line. The cable. The harness and swing. "They don't know what we know. They don't have a Katarina." I reach for my best friend's hand. She stands from where she sits on the floor, joining me. Ava stands, too. The three of us hold hands.

"Angelika," Aunt Brigitte says, "Sophie is right."

Mama doesn't say a thing. My grandfather, my uncle, my cousins, Katarina's family . . . everyone is quiet.

I press on, "Today we were supposed to decide when

to do this." I swallow. "Tomorrow. I think we should escape tomorrow. We need to go before anyone has time to get in the way."

Monika's friends.

Herr Becker.

We need to beat them all.

CHAPTER 41

For the last time in the East, I get ready for school. Last night, my declaration that Escape Night is happening was enough to persuade my aunt. From there, we swayed my grandpa . . . then my uncle. Katarina's parents, too. Finally, Mama agreed. She knows as much as anyone that it's too dangerous to stay. That we have everything to gain by taking this giant risk to leave.

And we're leaving today.

Mama's hug before she goes to work is the longest ever. "I'm proud of you," she says. "I'll see you soon."

As Mama goes down the hallway, I hope that the next time I see her she'll still be safe. I remind myself that I need to trust in what we've planned. It's a good plan.

And it's time to begin.

I set my tape trap and meet Katarina at the corner. The sky is a mixture of reds and oranges. The intensity of the colors somehow looks both ominous and hopeful. Together, we walk to school, see the same faces I've seen since first grade, and take a quiz, with the odd sensation of knowing my grade won't matter.

Katarina's papa should already be in the men's restroom at the House of Ministries. He snuck into the building during the morning rush, carrying the rope, handlebar, and swing seat in a large briefcase. We thought it'd look less conspicuous if a man was carrying it.

When it's time for lunch, Katarina and I go to my apartment. It's unsettling that the sky is still so vibrant, as if the universe knows this day is special, that we'll be escaping. I'm relieved when the tape is still there. Katarina doesn't want to eat alone at hers, knowing her mama and brother are on their way to hide. They are going to slip into the building during the commotion of the lunchtime hour. We figure Hans is young enough that no one will find it peculiar he's going into the women's restroom with his mama. Katarina's mama will also carry the cable in a bag. Women always have big bags. We hope no one will bat an eye.

Back at school, I mentally run through the rest of our escape plan.

Monika was *supposed* to go during the lunch rush,

too. But now she's not. A mixture of sadness and anger nearly has me snapping my pencil in half. Instead, my pencil twists out of my fingers and rattles against the floor.

Katarina widens her eyes at me, silently telling me to relax.

I'll try, but in equal parts, I can't believe Monika betrayed me and I also can't believe she's not coming today.

I can't focus on that.

At the final bell, I don't jump up out of my seat. I give myself a moment. Many people live here happily. I'm simply not one of them, especially now that Herr Becker made me sign away my life to him. As I leave the classroom, my teacher returns my quiz. An A. It feels oddly satisfying, even if it doesn't matter. Hopefully, I'll get an A on my biggest project of all—Escape Night.

Katarina and I walk home separately. She wants to see Anton one last time. His family's file has been destroyed, flushed, and is now swimming with the fishes in too many soggy pieces to ever put back together. I know that makes Katarina happy. But she's not happy about this goodbye, especially because he can't know it is forever. Everyone who knows us will be questioned after we escape. Anton can't know a single thing.

Monika will be questioned. She'll have to lie through her teeth to save herself, especially with Herr Becker already suspicious of her . . . and especially since I didn't help make him any less suspicious of her. Despite how mad I am at her, I hope she can do it. I suspect she'll always be watched, though.

I feel like I'm being watched right now. I feel like whoever is watching me can see the outline of the key in my pants pocket. Considering what's at risk and how dangerous today is, it's no wonder I'm paranoid. But as I approach my apartment door and see the tape disturbed, my legs nearly give out.

Someone has been inside since Katarina and I were here for lunch. I *know* I reset the tape when we left.

Who?

Why?

When?

And are they still here?

I've opened the door before to find Herr Becker.

My heart is beating too wildly and loudly to listen for any noises inside. Maybe I shouldn't go in. I'm not taking anything. All Mama took was the photograph of my papa. But I need to go in. I need to know if anyone will be following us.

Slowly, I turn the knob. The only light pours in from the windows. No one is on the couch. Nor in the kitchen. Or the bedrooms.

I'm alone. Whoever was here has left. But someone was definitely here. My Inventor's Box is open. I approach it as if there's a wild animal inside. Everything still appears to be in there. The problem is . . . after removing the handlebar, the rope, the swing, the purse strap, the tape, and the spool of cable, there is noticeably less in there. And I have a feeling Herr Becker knows it, that he's the intruder. He saw it overflowing with treasures the last time he broke into my apartment.

He knows for certain now that I'm up to something.

I backpedal from the box and out of my room.

I catch my breath, realizing I've been breathing hard. If my apartment has listening bugs, I bet it was even loud enough to hear.

Outside our windows, the colorful sky has been replaced by dark clouds. It looks like it could rain any moment, but I'm not supposed to go to the House of Ministries for another few hours.

I end up on the couch, the television on, trying to

pretend like this day isn't any different from any other Monday.

But it is. In a big, scary, exciting, and thrilling way.

I watch the clock more than I watch the television.

Finally, it's time.

I could throw up in the poor plant by the door again.

It makes me think of Erika's comment about throwing up bananas. That makes me smile. But a second later, I'm trembling again.

What if Herr Becker really does have suspicions?

What if one of Monika's friends is a spy, too, and told him, solidifying what he's already suspected?

What if I get to the House of Ministries and our plan has already blown up? I'm the very last person who is supposed to sneak into the restroom. There are five chances for someone to get caught before me. Not to mention that Katarina will be entering minutes before me with a huge bag with her bow and arrows inside. She insisted she should be the one to carry it. Grown-ups don't always see kids, especially when they aren't looking for them and busy with their own day.

But what if she's stopped and they check her bag?

Oh, this? Just a bow and arrow I need for a big meeting upstairs.

What were we thinking?

I'm torturing myself. I'm letting myself doubt, when I need to be trusting in myself.

I scream inside my head. I want to scream out loud. Instead, I take a deep breath. Patting my pocket, I double-check my bathroom key is still there.

For what will be the very last time, I leave my apartment, leaving the television and lights on.

It's a weird feeling knowing I won't ever be back. But either my feet will hit ground in the West, I'll be caught and imprisoned, or I'll be shot by the border guards.

I may believe in myself, but if there are three outcomes, that's only a 33 percent chance for the result I want.

CHAPTER 42

I don't like those odds. Not even a little. But I'm at the House of Ministries. Too early, in fact. My nerves pushed my feet faster and faster.

The good news is, as I walk past the large glass entrance doors, I don't see Katarina in the lobby. Nor do I see her outside. That means she's either in the restroom or she's been caught.

At least that's only 0.50 odds of our plan imploding, and I'd bet on my best friend every time.

I thought I could bet on Monika, too.

It's as if my mind conjures her because, all of a sudden, I spot her. She's on the bench down the street. Her knee bobs quickly. She's looking in the opposite direction.

I take a step backward. I don't want her to see me. I don't want to see her. But then her head slowly turns as if she's searching for someone.

Me?

Her friends?

Before, when I told her she wasn't welcome and Mama slammed the door in her face, Monika told us she'd keep anyone from getting in the way.

Is that why she's here? Is she keeping an eye out for her friends? I close my own eyes, wishing a lifetime of memories with Monika hadn't resulted in this moment. I wish she were already inside the House of Ministries. I wish we were hours away from escaping together.

Hadn't I imagined Escape Night countless times? This isn't how I dreamed it'd go.

I open my eyes. Monika is staring at me. Beside her on the bench, there's a newspaper. She lays a hand on it. Then Monika walks not toward me but away from me.

She wants me to get that newspaper. I know it.

Mama isn't here yet, and she's next to go inside the building. I have time to go see . . . if I can risk it.

I decide I have to.

In case anyone was watching Monika, I count to sixty. Then I do it again. It's the longest two minutes of my life.

Just as I begin walking toward the bench, a bus approaches.

Mama gets off, taking the steps down carefully. She couldn't come in her wheelchair. The front desk man, if it's the same one from Saturday, would recognize her chair. But will he recognize her? Most likely not. Most people only see her chair when she's in it.

Mama and I don't acknowledge each other. We don't even give each other the slightest of glances. But it's almost as if I can hear her in my head.

Be careful, darling.

You can do this, darling.

I'll see you inside, darling.

I watch from the corner of my eye as Mama enters the building.

She walks confidently toward the restroom. I lose her in a group of people exiting the lobby. A rush of panic courses through me. But I tell myself that no one recognizes Mama as the demanding woman who needed to use the restroom a few days ago and somehow has her own key this time.

What if I'm recognized?

What if someone sees me now, about to read a clandestine note?

I sink onto the bench, and I sit there. I let myself sit. And breathe. For a few moments, I people-watch, wary of any people watching me back. Then I reach for the newspaper, pretending to simply scan the headlines.

Inside the newspaper, I find Monika's note.

I'm sorry multiplied by infinity. I believe in you. This invention won't fail, and I won't fail you either. I hope to see you again someday.

My throat feels triple the size when I'm done reading. I clench my jaw, trying to keep the emotions off my face. Of course Monika knows I've been worried all along that my invention and plan won't work. But Monika is confident in me, so confident that she will make sure no one messes it up.

She made a mistake. She betrayed me. But I want Monika to know I forgive her.

On the newspaper, I scan for large lettering. At the top, I see an *M*. Near the right, there's an *E*. Down below, an *O*. And finally, I spot the *C*, the hardest letter to find in large type.

In each, I scratch and push until my finger creates a hole, poking out the letter.

I hope Monika will come back to this bench. I hope she'll see my anagram. I hope she knows I want her to come.

A honk startles me. Then a crash.

Two cars have collided in the street. Heads turn in that direction. I quickly close the newspaper and lay a hand on it as Monika had done. A breath later, I twist through the gathering onlookers toward the House of Ministries.

I mimic Mama's confidence, realizing I do feel like I can do this. A man even holds the door for me after he exits, though he does a double take.

"Visiting my papa," I say. I smile, liking that I've included my papa in this day, even if he's not actually here.

The man smiles. Within a few steps, I'm sure he's forgotten all about me, more interested in the commotion happening on the street.

Inside, I dodge a group of preoccupied men approaching the door.

I keep my head down, not looking at the front desk, not even looking to see if one of Herr Becker's secretaries is here. The last thing I want to do is make eye contact with anyone, especially them.

But a weird instinct has me looking up. My worst nightmare is unfolding. Coming into the lobby from the hallway is Herr Becker.

I gasp and grab a man by the back of his coat and throw myself behind him.

It backfires.

The man lets out a loud, "Hey!"

If Herr Becker is looking, I have no clue. My face is pressed into the man's back. He turns, taking me with him. I'm about to be the main attraction in the lobby. I release him and jump behind another group of men who are standing in a circle, animatedly talking. Their long trench coats form a wall.

"Becker!" one of them yells.

No!

This isn't happening.

I recognize Herr Becker's voice, greeting the man.

I'm hunched behind two side-by-side men, their coats hiding me.

But when they leave, I'll be hunched behind nothing, caught in the strangest of positions.

I have to chance leaving first.

Quickly as possible, I begin walking. I don't look back. I wait for Herr Becker's voice to fill the lobby, to fill my ears, to fill me with threats of how Mama is going to prison and how I'll go to a juvenile detention center.

I won't rat out the others. Maybe they'll get away unscathed.

But I don't hear his voice. I don't hear my name.

Somehow, I'm at the bathroom door. I fumble in my pocket for the key.

"Fräulein," I hear behind me.

I freeze.

I was so close.

Chapter 43

I slowly turn and find a woman standing behind me. She's holding up a key for the restroom. "I have mine out already," she says.

Relief must cascade off me, but the woman is already moving past me. "Allow me."

She unlocks the door and goes inside.

I quickly follow.

I'm in.

I can hardly believe it.

"So many toilets out of order," the woman mumbles. There are five stalls. Three of them have signs taped on the doors. "I should talk to the front desk."

"Oh," I start, the lie forming in my head as I say it, "I just heard someone complaining to them."

"Good," the woman says with a curt nod.

I practically dive into the last "working" toilet stall to wait out the other woman.

She takes a long time washing her hands. Too long. Is she wondering if I'm okay?

I flush and go to the free sink.

In the mirror, she smiles at me.

"Visiting my papa," I offer.

It worked before.

It works again.

It makes me smile again, too.

In no time, she dries her hands and leaves.

Holy cow. My armpits have never been so sweaty.

"Is everyone here?" I whisper.

Mama opens her door and pulls me into the tightest hug she's ever given me. "Katy?" I ask her.

"I'm here, Soph." Her voice comes softly from another stall. "My mama is here. Hans, too."

"Did your papa get in his restroom?"

"Yes," Katarina says. "I knocked on the shared wall when I got here. I worked it out with him ahead of time."

I smile. "Smart."

"We should get back in the stalls," Mama says. "Go in with Katy."

I do. She's sitting on the tank part of the toilet. Her bow and arrow case is between her and the wall. It's huge. I'm still so shocked she got it in here. She scoots over, making room for me.

Then we wait.

We wait for hours.

No one says a word, especially when the door opens. I twist to see through the crack, hoping it's Monika.

It's not.

My stomach rumbles. Katy's does, too.

Finally, Mama says, "Everyone should be gone by now."

Sunset was shortly after eight. My watch says it's after nine. Our family said they'd be on their side of the Wall from six o'clock on.

One by one, we leave our hiding places. Smiles don't last on anyone's face longer than a blink. We're happy to see one another but also nervous. Very nervous.

Mama stretches her arms and legs, a painful expression on her face. Katarina knocks on the shared wall, letting her papa know it's time.

"I'll peek," I whisper.

Mama shakes her head and pats her chest. As soon as she opens the door, she pops her head back in. But then she laughs. I quickly see it's only Katarina's papa waiting for us.

We all quickly leave the restroom and head toward the stairs. I can't help one last look back. Perhaps Monika hid somewhere in the lobby? But no, she's not here.

I lead the way. I'm the only one who knows these halls. At the stairs, I glance at Mama.

"I'll be okay," she says.

But within a few steps, I can tell she's not. "Lean on me," I say.

Mama shakes her head. "I can do this. I walked into the East. I'm going to walk out."

"Technically," I say, "you're going to glide out of here."

Mama smiles and leans on me. Together, we climb the stairs. One by one, we all step onto the roof.

A light drizzle is falling. The surface of the roof is glistening from the moon shining on the wetness. It's big enough still where it casts a glow. It's quiet, eerily quiet. I don't bother to prop the door. We're not going back.

"All right," I say to Katy. "Let's get everything ready."

The cable is stretched out straight.

The end of the cable is taped tightly to the fishing line.

The fishing line is already taped to the arrow.

Katarina practices pulling back an empty bow. Her arm shakes.

So far, no one has gone near the roof's edge. Katarina's mama hasn't even stood above a crouch, afraid she'll be seen. I creep toward the edge and look down. I don't see the dogs, but I remind myself they could be in the darker shadows. I peer across the death strip at the window in the Coca-Cola building. They're there. I see the movement of my family.

Uncle Rolf said he'd take care of attaching the cable. Leave that to him.

I turn back and motion to Katarina.

At a crouch, she creeps across the roof with the bow and arrow, staring at her feet the entire time.

She kneels beside me and whispers, "What if I mess up, Soph?"

"You won't. You mastered this on your roof."

"This roof is different."

"It is. There isn't a bird of prey watching us."

"It's raining."

"Do you think the arrow will slip?" I ask her.

"I don't know. I wish I could practice."

We both know she can't do that.

"I know you can do this, Katy."

Her head bobs but in an automatic way. "When I'm on my roof, I'm shooting *over* something. But there will be nothing underneath the arrow. I don't know why that's throwing me off."

Oh, there will be something underneath the arrow: the death strip. But it doesn't feel helpful to point that out.

"You can do it," I say again. "Do you believe me?"

Our eyes lock.

"Yes, I believe you."

I hold the bow and arrow for her so she can wipe her palms down her pant legs. She stands. In solidarity, I stand beside her. I want to duck back down. The rain mists my face. A breeze tosses my hair. I will it to stop. Katarina doesn't need wind added to the rain.

We stand there, feeling the eyes of the others on our backs.

Farther down the death strip a beam of light catches my eyes. It's coming from one of the towers. "That's normal," I say. "They are sweeping. They do it every night."

Mama told me about this. I'm glad she did.

Katarina watches the beam. They are sweeping on the opposite side of the guard tower.

I don't want to rush Katarina, but now's the time.

She positions her feet. She turns her body. She repositions her feet.

The arrow is on her bow.

Katarina straightens her right arm and raises the bow. Her left arm pulls back and back, until the bowstring touches the corner of her mouth.

I'm not breathing.

I'm not even sure Katarina is.

She blinks and moisture drips off her lashes.

Katarina releases the arrow.

It soars!

It soars over the death strip and out of the East!

Even though I can't see where it lands in the dark, I whisper shout, "You did it!" I whirl my best friend in a circle. Realizing ourselves, we both drop again to our knees. "You did it."

I imagine Uncle Rolf and my family searching for the arrow in the dark building.

Katarina lies backward, her arms and legs splayed out.

I laugh to myself and pick up the cable. In no time, I feel the tug on the fishing line. Uncle Rolf is reeling it in. The cable begins to go across.

It's working!

"Keep the cable lifted," I say to Katarina. It'll be easier for Uncle Rolf to pull. I grab our end of the cable to tie around the air vent. For this, I ask Katarina's papa for help, to make sure it's knotted correctly. The cable is a difficult material to bend, loop, and tie.

But we do it. The plan is going perfectly. Soon, the cable is taut. That means Uncle Rolf has attached it on his end. All I can do is trust he attached it well.

Together, Katarina's papa and I attach the seat, and I motion for everyone to join us. Mama is slow to get to her feet.

No one talks.

The rain picks up.

"How are we supposed to get on that thing?" Katarina's mama asks in a voice so low I almost can't hear it.

The air vent isn't high, which means the cable rests on the edge of the roof before angling down and across. Which means we'll need to go *off* the roof in order to get on the swing seat.

"I'll go first," Katarina's papa says. He edges closer to the cable and presses on it with his foot and bodyweight. It gives, but it doesn't buckle. Uncle Rolf has it secure. *This invention will work*, I tell myself.

Katarina's family hugs. Her mama is crying. Hans doesn't want to let his papa go. "We'll all be together soon. Over there." His smile is so reassuring.

He acts as if he's spelunking into a cave. He faces us, holds on to the roof's edge, and lowers himself over, his belly still against the building. With one hand, he reaches back, finds the chain for the swing. He then lowers himself onto the swing.

Katarina's papa lets out a sharp breath. "I'm on. It's holding. Hand me Hans."

Katarina's little brother wants no part of that.

But Mama and Katarina's mama coax him toward the edge. He's lowered onto his papa's lap. Like a spider monkey, he has his arms and legs wrapped around his papa.

We're all nodding in unison.

"See you over there," Katarina's papa says. With a push off the building with his feet, they begin to disappear into the darkness. Within seconds, we can barely see them. By the time they are going over the wall, they are mere shadows. The rope goes with them. Katarina and I both hold the remaining rope at separate spots. It's always good to have backup.

There's a tug. Together, we pull back the empty swing.

"Mama," Katarina says. "Go next."

"No," she says. "You go, Katarina. I want you safe."

"Go," I insist to my best friend.

There's no time to debate this. Herr Becker could show up at any minute. Monika's friends could burst through that door and bring unwanted attention with them. While that thought is horrifying, I still hope Monika is somehow on her way.

Katarina doesn't fight us.

I could cry I'm so happy to see Katy climb carefully and slowly onto the swing. With a kick, she's gone.

Mama puts her arm around me.

Katarina's mama goes next.

As soon as she disappears into the darkness, I grab Mama's hand. "Let me help you get on."

She looks like she wants to fight me, badly. We both know that'll leave me to escape last. If Mama wasn't feeling so lousy and her body didn't hurt so much from the stairs, I think she'd insist I go next. As it is, she can barely stand. Mama has little choice but to agree. I hug her. "I will be right behind you."

Holding on to Mama, I anchor her to the roof while she slowly lowers herself onto the swing.

She's on!

"I want to see you immediately," Mama says. Then I watch as she soars over the death strip.

But as she goes, Mama is suddenly illuminated. The watchtower's beam of light passes over her. In a heartbeat, she flies out of the light. The beam of light passes back and forth over the empty zip line, searching. She's gone. But they saw her. And now they see the zip line, too.

CHAPTER 44

I drop to my stomach.

Dogs begin barking.

There's yelling.

The beam of light is still passing over the zip line. Searching. Looking. Locating.

As quickly as I can, I begin pulling the rope. I imagine the seat jerking closer with each pull. I can't see it. It's too dark. I have to stop and lie against the roof when the searchlight passes over me.

They know there's an escape happening.

What they don't know is that I'm the only one left. Already, five people have escaped under their noses.

The rain has plastered my hair against my face. On my belly, I keep pulling and pulling.

Mama calls for me. Her voice is distant, shrill and panicked. "Sophie!"

Everyone is screaming for me now. There's no reason to be quiet anymore.

The dogs are frantic below me.

I pull the rope harder and faster. I see the swing! It glistens in the rain.

That's when there's a loud bang.

Right behind me.

Someone has burst through the door and onto the roof. The door is bouncing back from where it hit the side of the building.

Monika? Did she get my note? Did she solve my anagram? Has she come to escape, too?

No.

My stomach sinks at the sight of him. Herr Becker.

He's figured me out.

"I knew it!" he yells.

There's no doubting who I am, not with everyone panic-yelling my name.

Suddenly, shots ring out. They're shooting at the empty swing.

Herr Becker is running toward me. I leap to my feet. The swing's seat is close, but I only have seconds.

If I jump . . .

"Sophie!" Herr Becker yells. "Stop! Don't do it."

There's no way I'm stopping.

I dive for the seat. My belly hits first, and I almost topple over the seat. My hand finds the chain. I balance. I look like an arrow, my head sticking forward and my legs behind me. Except, friction slows me, and I stop moving forward.

Beneath me, the dogs jump. I see only the whites of their teeth and the reflection of their eyes, but I'm much too high. If I fall, I'll likely be as flat as a potato pancake before they have the chance to maul me.

I need to kick-start myself forward. I swing my feet, but I'm too far from the building to touch it to push off.

The spotlight blinds me, and I close my eyes. I'm suspended over the death strip. Stuck.

"Sophie," Herr Becker says more calmly. He's standing at the edge now. I twist back to see him. He's shaking his head, like a disappointed teacher.

There's a spotlight on him, too.

His arm is raised with his palm facing the tower.

Is he instructing them to hold their fire?

"Sophie . . . Sophie. I thought we were friends. How many have gone across?"

I don't answer him. I'm done answering him.

My family is still calling for me.

"Sounds like quite a few over there, Sophie."

I squint against the bright light. I can't see them. But they can see me. I know I'm breaking Mama's heart right now.

Herr Becker bends to retrieve the rope.

He tugs on it, and my seat jerks closer to him.

He tugs.

I jerk.

He tugs.

I jerk.

The way he grins sends a shiver toward me. He's enjoying this.

My feet hit the building.

But if Herr Becker has a flaw, it's underestimating me. I reach for the rope attached to the swing. I tug it. Hard. Slippery from the rain, the rope rips from his grasp. I yank again, and again. There's meters and meters of coiled rope. But it topples over the edge faster than Herr Becker can get a new grip on it.

With as much force as I can muster, I push off the building with my feet.

Momentum and gravity take hold of me.

I pick up speed.

I soar like Sophie Blanchard.

I hear Herr Becker screaming behind me.

The spotlight follows me.

A shot is fired.

Another.

The dogs bark.

I close my eyes.

I wait for the pain to come.

Instead, hands grab me. They pull me in. There's crying. There's so much crying. I open my eyes. Mama wipes the hair from my face. She kisses my forehead. My cheeks. Then so many people are hugging and kissing me that I don't know who is who.

I made it.

I'm in the West. Inside a building. Did I go through the large window?

I shot right through, just like Katarina's arrow must have.

A pang of sadness hits me that Monika isn't also hugging me. But I'm happy to be here, with my family. And Katarina. And her family.

We escaped. We invented a way across. We zip-lined from the East to the West, literally slipping through Herr Becker's fingertips. He once told me that all games have winners and losers. He said he never loses.

Well, today, he lost and I won.

I won. That makes this bittersweet moment even sweeter.

Grandpa hovers over me. "You're here, my bluestar."

I smile. "Mama guessed you'd call me that."

"Your mama knows me well," he says. "Even after all this time. And now we'll have all the time in the world to get to know each other, too."

"Let's go home," Aunt Brigitte says.

Yes, let's go home. A new future awaits me.

A NOTE FROM THE AUTHOR

Dear reader,

Thank you for joining me on Escape Night. I hope you enjoyed Sophie's story. Her character is fictional but is inspired by various actual events and real-life people who lived in East Berlin and West Berlin, separated by the Berlin Wall.

At the time of Sophie's escape, the Berlin Wall would have been standing for 4,271 days. And, it would take another 6,044 days to come down.

Can you imagine soaring over the death strip on a zip line? Sophie's escape is based on real life—two real-life moments, in fact.

In 1965, Heinz Holzapfel, his wife, and their young son escaped from the House of Ministries' roof. He went to the building for a meeting and hid his family in a toilet cubicle, hanging an *Out of Order* sign on the door. That night, from the roof, Heinz hurled a hammer with a rope attached to it over the death strip and the Wall. Helpers on the other side attached a metal cable to the hammer and the Holzapfels pulled it back to the roof. With a homemade harness made from a bicycle wheel axle, the family zip-lined one after another into the West. The border guards who witnessed it presumed the Stasi were smuggling agents into the West and didn't try to shoot them.

In 1983, two men named Michael Becker and Holger Bethke fired an arrow attached to a fishing line from an attic to a house on the other side. Holger's brother, who had already escaped years prior floating on an inflatable mattress, reeled in the line and connected a steel cable to the line. Michael and Holger pulled it back, then zipped across on wooden pulleys.

It was exciting to use elements from both these real-life plans.

During the years the Berlin Wall stood, there were various other successful escapes, many of which are mentioned in the novel, such as digging tunnels, tightrope walking, derailing a train, flying an ultra-light plane, driving in a tank, hiding in the trunk of a car, and even by flying a homemade hot-air balloon. There is a film that brings to life this last very creative escape called *Night Crossing* (rated PG).

How would you escape? Would you use science like Sophie?

People had different motivations for wanting to flee East Berlin. I can only speak to Sophie's, which was inspired by how jobs were not chosen, they were assigned and also how disabled people in need of help on a regular basis either had to stay with family or live in an institution, often in nursing homes for the elderly.

By 1989, the year the Berlin Wall came down, the Stasi had 10,000 known informants who were under the age of eighteen. This made up only 6 percent of the Stasi's known informants.

Kids, like Sophie, were forced to sign a declaration that swore them to secrecy. These first meetings between the Stasi and a child often took place in the principal's office. Children were asked to inform on neighbors, friends, teachers, and even family members.

Instead of the Stasi trying to physically harm people, they generally used psychological torture and mind games.

After Sophie's escape, I like to imagine her with her newfound family in the West, creating memories and making up for lost time. I like to imagine the

Fun-tastic Four inventing together and Sophie eventually taking a job in science. Or any other job she so desires now that she can choose.

If this storyline would've continued, I see Sophie and Katarina continuing to fight the oppression they faced in the East. Perhaps they'd scheme a way to rescue Anton or other families, like Sophie's papa had once done. Sophie's original Escape Night had included Monika. Sophie had to come to terms with Monika not joining them and Escape Night not going exactly as planned. However, in the moment Sophie coded *COME* in the newspaper, she forgave Monika and I picture Sophie later helping Monika escape, too. Monika would see her grandparents again.

Thank you again for reading. While researching and writing, I did my best to remain historically accurate wherever possible. All mistakes are my own. I'm very grateful to my authenticity readers Jennifer Keelan-Chaffins and Sara Stammnitz, my agent Shannon Hassan, my editor Olivia Valcarce, and copyeditor Jacqueline Hornberger for their efforts in also helping to make Sophie's story as realistic as possible. In telling her story, I enjoyed revisiting some of the (now older!) characters from *I Am Defiance*, once again remembering Sophie Scholl and her heroic actions from the Second World War, and creating new characters to bring the Cold War period of history to life.

J Walsh

Read Brigitte's story in another thrilling historical novel inspired by true events.

Don't miss *I Am Defiance*!

ABOUT THE AUTHOR

JENNI L. WALSH is the author of the companion to this book, *I Am Defiance*; the She Dared books: *Bethany Hamilton* and *Malala Yousafzai*; and many other books for young readers and adults. Her passion lies in transporting readers to another world, be it in historical or contemporary settings. She is a proud graduate of Villanova University and lives in the Philadelphia suburbs with her husband, daughter, son, and a handful of pets. Learn more about Jenni and her books at jennilwalsh.com or on YouTube at jennilwalshvideos, and follow her on Twitter, Facebook, and Instagram at @jennilwalsh.